Love Caus

MW01229367

Dedicated to my sorors who fell in love with Matt

Chapter 1

Matt

I stood in the mirror as my mother straightened my black bow tie. I was not nervous at all. I was happy. I was ready.

"I remember straightening your bow tie for your prom," she said to me.

"I remember too," I smiled.

"Now, I'm straightening it for your wedding."

She smiled and placed her hand on my cheek. I kissed her hand.

"Thank you for being so supportive."

"You're welcome. Now let me go check on my daughter-n-law to be."

I kneeled to straightened Braylon's bow tie. We were matching in black tuxedos. He stood in the mirror and smiled. I watched as he licked his finger before wiping it across his eyebrows and down his chin.

"That's my boy!" I laughed.

"We look, good Daddy," he said.

My mother laughed, "My boys are handsome."

James walked into the room as my mother was leaving out.

"Boss! Today is the day!"

"Yeah, it is," I said gripping his hand and we embraced.

"I am happy for you!" he said to me. "I remember when you first heard her voice."

"Yeah," I said. I thought back to the day we checked in at the airport for our flight. I closed my eyes and exhaled. I opened them and looked at James. "That's my lady."

"Your soon-to-be wife..."

"I do like that better."

We heard loud knocks on the men's dressing room door.

"Come in," I said.

The door flew open. Asia rushed in carrying Madeline. She was screaming at the top of her lungs.

"Daddy! I want my daddy!"

My baby girl was two years old. She was walking. She was talking. Her favorite word was daddy and I loved every moment of it.

"Take this spoiled brat! We can't finish getting ready because she is screaming!"

Madeline reached out to me. I took her from Asia's arms. I rubbed her back.

"What's wrong with my princess? You look so pretty in your dress, stop crying."

Asia folded her arms in the black robe she was wearing, "She's rotten! That's what! Keep her with you until the wedding starts!"

"Isn't she a flower girl?" I laughed. "She has to come back with you all."

Asia laughed. "Brooke thinks she is a flower girl! She showed out last night at rehearsal because her daddy was not there! We don't know what she is going to do."

I kissed Madeline on her caramel vanilla cheek. She was my twin. I couldn't deny her. She laid her head on my shoulder. Asia rolled her eyes. She licked her tongue out at Madeline.

"Bye brat!"

"You better leave my baby alone," I laughed.

I sat down in a nearby chair with her. I straightened out her dress.

"Will you throw flowers for daddy?"

She shook her head no and squeezed my neck. I laughed and rubbed her back.

At a normal wedding, the groom would walk out first with the pastor and his best man. Well, the officiant, James, and I had a flower girl with us! Madeline was my shy baby. As soon as she saw the crowd of people, she was almost climbing up my leg. I picked her up. She buried her head in my chest.

Soft music began to play. Our wedding was starting. Reality was sinking in. I took a deep breath and focused on the aisle. My father was there. He and my mother had no ill feelings. They settled their differences. I do believe my successful eye surgery and the birth of Madeline helped them get it together. My father was her escort. He wasn't as handsome as I was in his tuxedo. He was alright! My mother was beautiful in her sophisticated gold dress. I smiled at the sight of the two walking down the aisle. They even sat at the table together.

Believe it or not, my soon-to-be mother-n-law was present at our wedding. Naomi came to see Madeline after she was born. She and Brooke were able to talk. Brooke forgave her for not believing her and shutting her out when she divorced Carson.

My siblings better not had missed my wedding day! Melvin and Mackenzie appeared. I smiled at the duo. My baby sister was radiant. She was not the type to dress up. She hated dresses! I was happy I was able to see her glow again. I was happy that she did it for me.

My little overprotective sister who thought she was my big sister smiled at me as she walked down the aisle in the flowing rose red dress. The road to Melissa and Brooke getting along was not easy. It was bumpy at first. They managed to get over the humps. I was happy two of my favorite women were getting along.

My little sister from another mother was a bridesmaid. I was hoping Phayla did not drop the tears as I saw them filling her eyes. I did not want her to ruin the red dress. I knew she was happy for me and Brook.

You guessed it right! Asia was the maid-of-honor! Brooke was torn between her and Phayla. She told me she chose Asia. Not because she was her best friend, but because she was the one who told her to go on the first date with me. Brooke felt she and I would not have been together without encouragement from Asia.

I had a big influence on Braylon! It did not surprise me when the boy took his time to stroll down the aisle. I even saw the boy smiling at cameras and raising his eyebrows. He just couldn't be the regular ring bearer! I couldn't be mad at anyone but myself.

My angel was growing! She was getting a little height on her! She was just as sassy as her mother! Daddy was not handling it well! I did not want Cassidee to grow up. We were done taking trips to the hospital! That was a blessing. She like Braylon was a character! She knew she was pretty! Daddy had to tell her every day! I was raising two young queens and a king. She waved at people as she dropped her flowers. She even stopped and smiled at a camera. I was embarrassed.

The music stopped. A new tune started. Me being me, I had to have a surprise at our wedding for Brooke. I did not tell her I changed the song she would be walking down the aisle to.

Brooke

I froze at the sound of Brian McKnight's "Never Felt This Way." My heart was so full. I closed my eyes and reminisced about the day Matt played the song for me. He had his sight back. I came home to a path of roses greeting me at the door. I followed the roses to the living room. There was a note on the couch. I smiled and picked it up. I read it.

"There was once upon a time when I could only listen to you. Now it's your turn."

The song then began to play. I sat down on the couch and listened to the song. He walked into the living room after the song ended with two glasses and a bottle of champagne. I smiled and said to him,

"Baby, it's your birthday and you're doing things for me."

He leaned in and gently kissed me. "I have never felt the way I feel now on any birthday. The first birthday I can see and spend it with my beautiful fiancé."

I rubbed my hand down his face. "I am glad I can spend today with you. I am looking forward to more. Happy birthday."

I heard Todd ask me, "Brooke. Are you okay? Are you ready?"

I nodded my head yes. I could hear the double doors opening. I slowly opened my eyes. I began to raise my head. I looked around the room. There were so many people there. I thought back to when I left home. I did not have the love or support that was in the room on my wedding day. I recognized my employees. You heard me right! I was promoted to the hiring manager at the airline. Many of Matt's colleagues were there. I joined arms with Todd. We began to walk down the aisle.

My eyes locked with Matt's. He smiled. He ran his hand down his face. I knew what that meant. Just as I thought, a tear fell from his left eye.

Matt

My love was beautiful without the wedding dress. She was gorgeous in a pair of sweatpants and a t-shirt with tennis shoes! She was exquisite in the wedding dress. It fit her body perfectly. She was still a fan of the fitted dresses. I became a fan over the years. I even found myself buying her fitted clothes. If she liked them, I loved them!

She chose not to be traditional. I was not surprised! Her dress was not white! I mean it wasn't like either one of us was pure! I could not wait to get her out of the dress! But back to her dress, it was not a traditional one because she was far from traditional. One thing I loved about her! She had no problem with being different! If she was a glass of champagne, she would be the smooth kind that slowly touched your soul. The jewels on the dress would be the glistening bubbles that fizzed as the champagne sat. The mermaid fit started with a perfect touch at her bust and eased down until it flared at the bottom.

She stopped in front of me. More than one tear was falling. I never thought I would see my wife walk down the aisle to me. The officiant asked, "Who gives this woman away." Todd responded,
    "I do."

Brooke

I was never prepared for the things Matt said to me. As much as I tried to prepare myself for his vows, I knew I still was not ready. The day we decided to write our vows, I cried! I knew I was not going to be any good on this day! I listened as he made his vow to me.

Matt

Before I could make a vow to you, I had to make a vow to God. I vowed to make him first in my life. If I could not make him first in my life, I could not have you. You were and are the most precious gift from him. I was not able to fully have you the way he ordained me to have you if he was not in my life. It took me some time, but I realized I had to rededicate myself to him. Once I did that, he allowed me to receive the blessings he had for me. He blessed me with my sight to be able to see you and to love you the proper way. He blessed me with my sight to see our children and those to come. He blessed me with my sight to live life according to his word. Marriage is of God. I am vowing to live according to his word with you and for the rest of our lives.

Brooke

Asia handed me a tissue. I took the tissue and wiped the tears that were flowing down my face. I took a deep breath before reciting my written vows.

"I was not used to the truth before you. My life had been a lie and I was not a fan of being truthful. I thought I could run from the truth all my life. That changed when I met you. Even though I was afraid to date a blind man, the truth was, I fell in love with you. I fell in love with you before our first anniversary. It was more like when you accepted my children. I knew if you loved them, you had to love me. I was still dishonest about my life. You did not know it and when you discovered my secret, you still came back. I knew I had to be honest. I was honest and you stayed. I am vowing to be honest. I am vowing to love you the way you have loved me. I am vowing to be there through situations. The good and the bad. For the rest of our lives."

Chapter 2

Matt

I gave Brooke all she wanted and more. All she had to do was ask. There were times where she did not have to ask. I had no problem with spoiling her. She asked for a Caribbean location for our honeymoon. St. Lucia it was! Beaches, hiking, trails, and waterfalls! We enjoyed our time. We enjoyed it so much, neither one of us wanted it to end. We had to get back to our children. Life as a married couple was about to begin. I was ready!

I stepped off the elevator in a pair of khaki slacks with a light blue dress shirt and a navy blue tie. My favorite brown dress shoes kept my stride going! I couldn't forget the navy socks with light blue polka dots. James met me as I was walking to Phayla's office for updates.

"Well! Look who is back!"

I laughed. "Back and energized!"

"She got you more energized than the bunny huh!"

"Married man privileges! You wouldn't understand!"

James laughed. "I may understand sooner than you think."

I stopped walking. James hadn't told me he was dating.

He laughed. "Don't look at me like that man."

"So, who is this woman you're dating?"

He continued to laugh. "I did not say I was dating."

I gave him a side-eye. "You said I may understand sooner than I think. That implies you are dating."

James laughed. "You assumed."

"Okay. I see how it is."

I knocked on Phayla's door. "Good morning!"

"Hey!" She got up from her desk and came to the door. We shared a hug.

"Brooke sent me pictures! I see you all enjoyed yourself!"

"We did," I said. "We almost did not come back!"

"Well, I'm glad you did. Asia and I had the hardest time with Madeline! You have got to stop spoiling that child."

"My baby is not spoiled! She is just well loved!"

"Yeah, whatever!" Phayla pushed James. "Did he give you updates or naw?"

"He did not give me any updates about the company. He mentioned something else."

"You're supposed to be the assistant!" She shook her head at James. "Promote me already! Fire this guy!"

James gave Phayla a fake smile. "Women!"

"Get smacked," smirked Phayla.

"So aggressive! You need a man in your life!"

Phayla laughed. "Boy! Shut up! Matt let me give you the updates he was supposed to give you."

"Maybe you can update me on who he is dating too."

"I slick threw up in my mouth," said Phayla.

I laughed. James was not laughing. That made me laugh even more.

Phayla teased James. She nudged me and winked. "Dating! Who are you dating James?"

"Let's just give him the updates," said James brushing past us and walking into Phayla's office.

We both laughed and joined him. We sat down in the chairs in front of her desk. Phayla sat behind her desk. She pulled out a file.

"I have applications and resumes from potential managers for our new location."

She opened the file. She handed me resumes. I began to scan the resumes.

"I know you are going to look through them. I already have one picked," said Phayla.

James then said, "I have one too."

"You just like her because you think she is fine."

"She seems to have a nice attitude. Maybe if we hire her, you can learn from her," snapped James.

"Okay!" I said trying to get the two to stop. "I am going to take these and look over them. If I see a person with the experience to do the job, I will still bring in your picks for their second interview with me."

"Thank you!" said Phayla. She rolled her eyes at James.

I was sitting behind my desk looking through the resumes. I thought about Brooke. I decided to shoot her a text.

"Hey, Mrs. Franklin. I just thought about you."

It wasn't long before she texted back.

"Hey, Mr. Franklin! Aren't you sweet! You're always on my mind too! Love you."

I smiled. I got back to reviewing the resumes. After about two hours of reviewing, I had two potentials I wanted to interview. I headed back to Phayla's office to inform her to add the women to the list.

"Got that one," she said.

"Roslyn Gladdon, add her too," I said.

I watched as Phayla stopped writing. She looked up at me and shook her head.

"No," she said.

I eyed her. I knew she knew something. I eyed her back.

"Don't start with the questions, just no. I know you have a backup."

"I do not," I said. "What is it?"

Phayla leaned back in her office chair. "We have been business partners for a long time. Just trust me."

I wanted to know why she did not want me to interview the young lady. I sat down in a chair in her office.

Phayla then said, "Oh God! You have sat down! I don't want to talk about it."

"If you can't tell me what is wrong with the girl, I don't see anything wrong with interviewing her."

"It would not be good for the business. I ran her background check."

I laughed. She was lying.

"You know I am not going to pick someone without running a check behind you. She's clean. Spit it out."

Phayla rolled her eyes, "Nothing! Okay! I'll call her in for the final interview."

"Thank you" I smiled.

"Yeah! Bye!"

Brooke

My mother moved to Dallas after Madeline was born. She felt she needed to be there for her grandchildren. I respected that. She and I worked on our relationship. It was not perfect. It was getting better. Her relationship with the kids was great. I allowed them to visit her. She even picked them up from school some days.

I used my key to her house to open her front door. She was in the kitchen cooking.

"Hey," I said to her.

"Hey babes," she said leaning in to accept my hug before continuing to stir in the pot of pasta. I took a bottle of water from her fridge and sat down at her table. Madeline was the first to run into the kitchen.

"Mama!"

I smiled and picked up my youngest. I kissed her on her cheek. Braylon came into the kitchen wearing his school uniform, black pants, and a yellow shirt.

"Hey, Mama!"

"Hey, Son! How was your day?"

"It was good!" he smiled.

"That's good! I'm going to look at your report when we get home!"

"I have a good report!" he smiled.

"We will see," I said eyeing him. "Where is your sister? Go tell her it's time to go."

"She's writing a letter," he said to me.

"Writing a letter?"

My mother then chimed in. "She is practicing letter writing for school. She finished her homework. I told her to just leave the extra ones here. She wanted to practice more. You know how she is. She can't mess up!"

I smiled. My mother was right. Cassidee was growing and loved school. She hated to miss a problem or get one answer wrong on her assignments.

I was driving home. My children were in the backseat. Madeline sat in her car seat in the middle of Braylon and Cassidee. I wanted to know more about their day at school. Talking about their day was our normal routine.

"Cassidee, you all are learning how to write letters at school huh?"

Cassidee was staring out the window. "No. We are learning multiplication."

"What?" I asked her. "Your grandma said you all were writing letters."

I could see her in my rear-view mirror. Her eyes became bigger. She turned from the window. She looked down at her feet and said,

"Oh yeah! We are!"

"Who did you write a letter to?"

She kept looking down at her feet.

"A friend in my class. They had to write one back."

She then looked up and smiled at me in the mirror.

Matt

I knew Phayla was not going to call my choice back for the second interview. I did it myself. I was right! She had not received a phone call back. I was trying to figure out why Phayla did not call her back. She did not appear to have an attitude on the phone. She was very polite. The young lady was very articulate.

I scheduled her interview on a different day than the other interviews. I scheduled it during Phayla's lunch period. I was hoping the interview would go well. I had planned on hiring the young lady. Her references cleared! Her resume was on point! She had the experience! She had more experience than the other applicants.

Her interview was scheduled for 12:15 p.m. I noticed the time was 11:45 a.m. I headed toward the receptionist's desk. I wanted to catch her before anyone else could. She stepped off the elevator at 11:50 a.m. She was on time! That was more points added to the resume and experience! That told me she would be on time for work. Her outfit was a plus too! She was younger than the other applicants. Her age said a mini skirt with a tight button-down that would most likely have her cleavage all out with a pair of 6-inch heels. Her resume said a black skirt suit with a white blouse and kitten heels. She matched the resume! No colored hair! Just a natural look pulled back into a ponytail.

I introduced myself to her.

"Welcome to Lady in Red. I am Matt Franklin. You must be Roslyn."

The young lady shook my hand with a firm grip. "I am. Nice to meet you."

"Same here, we can head this way for your interview."

I sat down behind my desk. She sat in a chair in front of my desk. I was not one to always start with a formal interview. I took the informal approach. It would help me get a real feel for the candidate.

"So, tell me about yourself. Keep in mind, I have reviewed your resume."

She smiled. "I am from here. Born and raised. I have two older siblings. I have a dog. My favorite color is green. I am a Pisces."

I was hoping that she would tell me some fashion or retail experience. I gave her one more time to redeem herself.

"What made you apply for this position?"

"You," she said.

I thought I heard her wrong. I had to ask her again. "What made you apply for this position?"

"You," she said again.

Yeah, I heard her right.

"I thank you for your honesty. However, you can't be here for me. I am married. We are going to go ahead and end the interview. Thank you for your time."

Roslyn then said to me, "Oh! I am so sorry! I did not know. Now I feel crazy." She lowered her head. "I do want the job. I read about you in an article online. I didn't read where you were married. If I were, to be honest, I came here intending to get you and the job. I guess I messed up the second one."

I smiled at her. "Let me escort you back up to the front."

I did not know exactly why Phayla did not want to interview the young lady. I did have a feeling she knew the young lady was attracted to me. I was not going to tell her I scheduled the interview. I would not ever live it down!

Brooke

The kids were outside playing in the backyard. I was doing my regular Saturday cleaning. I needed to wash linens. I took the linens from Braylon's bed. I placed them in a hamper and headed to Madeline's room. Cassidee's room was last. I removed the pink comforter from her bed. Next was the single sheet. I pulled back the fitted sheet. Folded papers caught my attention. There were three folded pieces. I unfolded one. It was a letter. I started to read it. I could not believe what I was reading. I did not want to believe what I was reading. I tossed the letter down. My breathing picked up. I tried to calm myself down. I unfolded a second letter. I read it. A tear fell down my face.

"Brooke! Sweetheart!" I heard Matt calling out to me. I could hear him coming down the hall. I hurried and wiped my face. I took the letters and hid them in the comforter.

"In here!"

He stood in the doorway. "I am about to head out to the store. Do you need anything?"

"I'm fine," I said placing the fitted sheet into the hamper.

Matt could read me better than anybody.

"Are you okay?"

I was close to a panic attack. I couldn't tell him what was wrong. I would have passed out.

"I'm just a little tired."

"Well rest," he said walking over to me and taking me in his arms.

I smiled. "The kids will be back in later. I will have to get them ready for baths."

He rubbed his hand down my face. "When I get back from the store, how about you rest. I will finish up around here."

"Thank you," I said.

Matt returned home from the store. He did as he said he would. He picked up where I left off with the cleaning. I told him I was going to take a shower. I went into our master bathroom in my robe. I closed the door behind me. I locked it. I cut the shower on. I reached into my robe pocket and pulled out the letters. I needed to finish them. I sat down on the toilet and I read each one. The more I read, the angrier I became. The more I read, the more I realized Matt could never find the letters.

I managed to remain calm throughout the next day. Even though I held it together, I needed to talk to someone! I invited Asia for lunch the next day. I told her I wanted to have lunch in a private secluded place. She asked about my house. No way! She told me to meet her at her house. That was fine. I found myself beating on her door. I needed to get things off my chest.

"Girl!" she said opening the door. "Your knocks don't say let's have lunch!"

"I lied!" I pushed past her and walked into her house.

"You're here without Phayla. I know you're lying! What's going on? You must don't want her to know?"

"She would tell Matt. He would lose it! I need to handle this myself!"

"Handle what?"

I threw myself onto her couch. I took the letters from my purse and handed them to her.

"What are these?"

"Just read them!"

Asia took the letters from me and sat down next to me. I covered my face. I could hear the paper rattling. She was silent for a minute. She then lost her cool!

"Girl! What in the hell! I did not even have to get past the dear part!"

"I know. I know!" I said getting up from her couch.

I could not help but pace. "I wonder if there are more?"

"Where did you find these?"

"In her sheets!"

"She knows to hide them! Why do I feel like somebody is helping her?"

I stopped and eyed Asia.

"I don't even want to think about that! Who? Why?"

"She is writing back."

"That is what is confusing me!" I said. "She knows the truth!"

"Have you talked to Matt?"

"I'm going to handle this one on my own."

"You should talk to him!" said Asia.

"Do you want me to handle it or do you want him to handle it?"

Asia then said, "Well, you have a point there. Wait! What is your plan?"

I sighed. "I am going to get to the bottom of it. I can't let Matt find out. He will kill everybody!"

Asia sighed. "Okay! Look! When are we going?"

"We?" I asked her.

Asia stood up from her couch. "You aren't going by yourself!"

"How do you know I am going?" I asked her.

"You will do anything to protect your children. That's what a mother does!"

"No more running," I said to her.

"Exactly," she said. "So, when are we going?"

Chapter 3

James

I stuck my head into Phayla's office. She was on the phone. She motioned for me to come in. I walked in and closed the door behind me. I listened as she conducted business. I could tell she was speaking with the contractor we hired to renovate one of the old boutiques. I waited for her to finish. Once she finished, she placed the office phone on the receiver.

"What's up?"

She turned back to her desk.

"How has your day been?"

"Good. What's up?"

"Have you been to lunch?"

"Yeah. What's up?"

"Nothing!" I snapped.

Phayla leaned back in her chair. "You good?"

"You keep asking me what's up. Why can't I just come in here and talk to you?"

Phayla folded her arms. "Well, because you always want something."

"That's not true," I said to her.

"Very much so," she said.

"Name a time," I challenged her.

Phayla rolled her eyes. "Okay, well you're always getting on my nerves."

"We have worked together for years! You make me sick too. Especially when we lived at Matt's together."

She laughed. "No! You had your side of the house but stayed coming to my side."

I laughed. "I mean, you were the only person besides him that I was with 24/7. We had some good times in the house."

Phayla lowered her head. "Um, I need to get back to work."

Why was she acting strange? Matt was not in the room.

"Since when do you not like reminiscing about the times we had?"

"We have talked about this," she snapped.

"No, you never want to fully admit your true feelings," I said to her.

"Matt has his sight back now."

"I will handle him. I do not want to sneak around with you anymore. We did that when he was blind. Our relationship is not going to interfere with the business. Besides, he did not build this alone. He is happy. You deserve to be happy. I deserve to be happy. We deserve to be happy."

I watched as tears filled her eyes. "It's more than about the business."

I knew Phayla. She had been responding differently to me lately. We always acted as though we could not stand each other in front of Matt. Her demeanor was different.

"There's somebody else huh?" I asked her.

She did not have to answer me. I got up from the desk. I was angry. I could have torn a hole in her office wall.

"You're mad for what!" she yelled out. "You just came in here today and tell me you're done sneaking around with me! You should have told me this years ago!"

I yelled back at her "You never allowed me to!"

There was a knock on her office door.

"Are you all good in there?" asked Matt.

Phayla hurried and wiped her face. I straightened my face.

"You good?" I asked her.

"Just open the door," she said throwing herself down in her office chair.

Brooke

The silver BMW stopped in a parking spot. I stared out the window. I could only think about Cassidee.

"You want me to go with you?" asked Asia.

I sighed. "I got it."

Asia lowered her head. "I'll be waiting for you."

I got out of the car and headed toward the building. I walked through the door. I had never been there before. I did not know how things worked.   Asking someone was not in the plan.   I followed the actions of the other people. There was a line leading to a window. The people were signing a piece of paper. When I made it to the window, I saw it was a sign-in sheet. I read the columns. I had to put the time and my name. I did not want to fill in the last box. I knew I had to. My hand shook as I filled in the box.   After completing the sheet, I followed the line of people in front of me.   There were two metal detectors. I had to remove my shoes. I did not have anything with me. I could not bring any items into the building. I stepped through the metal detector. I was clear. I had to be checked a second time. I thought it was procedure until I heard one of the officers say it was because of the content in the last box. I also had to be placed in a different line. There were only two other people in the line. The line next to us had more than forty people in it. I wanted to turn around and go back to the car. Thoughts of my baby then came to me. I had to go.

The three of us in the line were taken to a small hallway of windows. We were told to sit at the end and skip a seat. I was the last person to sit down. I stared down at the white counter. I wanted to vomit. I had to get it together. It was almost time. I heard another door open. It wasn't the door in the room where we were seated. I slowly looked up. I made direct eye contact with Carson. He sat down in the chair. I took the phone from the wall. He did not move. He only stared at me. I did not look away. He tilted his head to the left. He sat back in the chair. He folded his arms. I squinted my eyes at him. After he saw that I was not leaving, he took the phone from the wall.

"Why are you here?" he asked me.

"You tell me," I snapped.

He rubbed his hand down his face. "I don't have time to play these games with you."

"It ain't like you got somewhere to be," I said shrugging my shoulders. "Now me on the other hand, I can walk out of this door and find somewhere to go to make things a lot harder for you."

"You act like I am not in here for life," he smirked. "What else you are gone do to me?"

"You know what you're doing," I snapped. "It needs to stop."

"You're talking to the wrong person."

"No, I am talking to who I need to talk to," I snapped. "I don't know how you're doing it. I just know it needs to stop."

Carson laughed. "You know what? You try to sound all bad. When the sad part is you're scared to talk on this recorded line."

I smirked. "Don't write my daughter again."

Carson continued to laugh. "What is the threat if I keep writing her?"

I laughed. "Just like you think you have everything in a bag because this phone call is being recorded. I too have everything taken care of."

I stood up. Before placing the phone back on the receiver, I said my final words.

"Don't write my daughter again."

Carson smirked. "You just remember this. I did not write her first."

Asia was standing outside of the car when I made it back. I knew she was waiting for me to give her the details of the conversation with Carson.

"You were right," I said to her.

"Somebody is helping her write the letters huh?"

I threw my body against the car in disbelief.

"He told me I was talking to the wrong person."

"He didn't say who was helping her?"

"It's Carson! He lives for mind games! No, he didn't tell me!"

"Do you think Cassidee will tell you?"

I did not want to question Cassidee about writing letters to Carson. If it bothered her, she would tell me. Unless she was told not to tell me.

Phayla

Every Friday I started my weekend off with the girls. We would meet at my house for crafting and wine. It was a relaxing way to end our busy week. We were sipping our wine while we painted miniature wooden houses at my kitchen table.

"I am so glad to be away from Terry and TJ!" said Asia.

Brooke and I laughed. Asia continued. "I think I want to have a little girl."

"You can come to get one of mine! I don't know why you won't!"

Asia cut her eyes at Brooke. "My baby is a big girl now and you can keep the tasmanian."

Brooke laughed. "Madeline is not that bad!"

Asia cut her eyes again. "Honey! She is too!"

"Have you been trying?" I asked Asia.

"Trying ain't the word! I should be pregnant every 9 months!"

"Well excuse us!" I laughed. "We need no details."

Asia laughed. "Speaking of details! When are you going to start back getting the insides of your car detailed!"

Brooke almost spits her wine across the table. I eyed Asia.

"What?" laughed Asia. "I am just saying! At one point you were all happy and for like the last month you've been all down and sad."

"You're dramatic! I have not. No man is or was detailing me," I said.

"Stop with the lies! Just because you won't ever disclose him does not mean we don't know!"

"If I had a man, you two would be the first to know."

Asia laughed. "Okay! So, tell us who was detailing you inside and out. Whoever it was, he had you all glowing on the inside. The wax job had that body and outfits banging. Now you're dressing like Raggedy Ann!"

I rolled my eyes and kept painting my house.

"You don't have to tell us," said Asia. "It's okay! I know it was a man around!"

My text message alert sounded. Brooke and Asia eyed one another. I knew they were about to start. Brooke took the first jab at me.

"Ma'am, it's almost midnight!"

Asia did not bother to let her finish.

"Who is that?"

I ignored them. I picked up my phone. James was texting. Of course, his name was not saved in my phone as James. It was saved as five red hearts. The number of letters in his name.

"Hey, I want to see you."

I sighed before texting him back.

"What's up. I am hanging with the girls."

"I'll be up," he replied. "Just text me when you're done."

"Will do," I replied.

I chose not to text him. I called him instead. I did not think he would be up at 2:00 a.m. He was up. He told me he was headed to my place. I sat on my living room couch under a blanket. I did not have to get up when I heard his car pulling into my driveway. He had a key. He walked into my living room in a pair of blue pajama pants with a black hoodie. He sat down on the couch next to me.

"We need to talk," he said to me.

"Okay," I said.

"I don't think you are seeing someone else."

I sighed. "James, you are not serious. You never were serious."

He looked into my eyes and said, "I have always been serious with you and you know it. You're the one who felt as though Matt would fire you if he found out we were together. I always told you I would handle it."

"You never handled it!" I yelled.

"Oh! So, I was supposed to read your mind? You never told me you wanted me to handle it."

"I should not have had to!"

"Well I told you at the office I would handle it. I am telling you now. I will handle it! I will call him right now! That's how serious I am."

"I can't," I said.

James then said to me, "I know it's not someone else! You would have taken your key from me in the office. You would have not responded to my text. What is the real reason?"

I knew why I did not want to pursue things with James. I was not willing to share it with him. James reached into his hoodie pocket.

"I wanted to do this a different way. I don't know any other way to show you how serious I am."

I knew what he was about to pull from his pocket. I begged him not to.

"Please don't."

I closed my eyes. Tears fell. I opened them and there was the small black box I was dreading to see. He opened it revealing a rather large diamond ring.

"This is how serious I am."

"This is why I can't."

James lowered his head.

"You don't want to marry me?"

I wiped my tears as they fell.

"My reasoning goes beyond Matt's opinion. You have been living your life. You are much older than me. I am just starting mine. I am not ready to stop. I am at the peak of my career. No, I don't want to get fired. Sooner or later, I don't even want to be working for Matt. I want to be working for myself!"

"I know all of your goals," he said closing the box. "I would not dare stop you from reaching them.

You know that. Well, I thought you knew that. My age, I am not even going to address it. It wasn't stopping you before." He took my house key from his keys and placed it on my living room table.

"I'm done begging you."

He got up from my couch and walked to my front door. He did not say another word to me. He opened the door and I heard it close.

Brooke

Matt and I loved to take the kids out for dates. If Braylon and I were out, he was most likely with the girls. It was my turn to have a date with the girls. They wanted to go to the movies and out to eat. It was a date! After the movie, we went to have their favorite! Pizza! We were sitting at the table eating pepperoni pizza. I stared at Cassidee. Carson's words echoed through my mind.

"I did not write her first. You're talking to the wrong person."

I did not want to question Cassidee. As much as I did not want to, I needed to.

"Cassidee, you know I love you right?"

She smiled and took a bite of the pepperoni slice of pizza.

"Yes, I know you love me. I love you too Mama."

"You know it's good, to tell the truth, right?"

"Yes ma'am," she nodded.

I smiled at her. "That's my big girl. If I ask you something and you tell me the truth, you know I won't be mad at you because I love you right?"

"Yes Mama," she said picking up her cup and drinking from her straw. I watched the red punch travel in the straw into her mouth and back down into the cup. She placed the cup down on the table.

"Who have you been writing the letters to?"

Cassidee lowered her head. She slumped down in the booth.

"Dad."

"Thank you for telling me the truth. Now if I ask you more questions, will you tell mama the truth?"

"Yes ma'am," she said.

"Has someone been helping you?"

She nodded her head yes. I was afraid to ask her who. I was ready to find out for myself. I lowered my head and stared at the pizza in front of me.

"Grandma," she said.

I immediately rose my head. She slowly lifted hers. She looked at me. Her eyes watered.

"She told me to tell you that I was learning to write letters in school. She told me to hide them. I didn't know where to hide them. I hid them in my bed covers."

"Did you want to write him?"

"No. She told me that it was the right thing to do because he was my real dad. Are you going to tell Daddy? I don't want him mad at me."

Tears filled my eyes. I could not let them drop. I held on to them tight.

"You don't have to write him if you don't want to and Daddy is not going to be mad at you."

"I don't want Daddy to think I don't love him. I love him. I was just doing what Grandma told me."

"I know sweetheart. Your daddy knows you love him. He loves you too. If you always tell the truth, Daddy will always love you."

My children were in the car, I couldn't speed. I was anxious to get them to Asia's house. I was ready to speed to my mother's house. Asia came out of the house before I could pull into her driveway. She came to the car and got the girls.

"Are you going to be okay?" she asked me.

"No, but I will be." I placed my car in reverse.

I walked into my mother's house and slammed the door behind me. She was sitting at her kitchen table with my mother-n-law. That was just great! Now she was going to know Cassidee was writing to her felon of a father!

"Hey babes," said my mother.

"Hey Mama," I said eyeing her. "Hey, Katherine."

Katherine reached out and grabbed my hand. I was staring at my mother. Katherine gently rubbed the top of my hand. She could tell I was upset. She knew me more than my mother. It was sad.

"Katherine, can I please speak with my mother?"

"I think I'm going to stay," she said calmly to me. She kept rubbing my hand.

"Katherine please," I asked her.

Katherine would not leave. There was no way Matt could find out Cassidee was writing Carson. I knew Katherine was staying there for me. She and I had a great relationship. She also knew every detail about my relationship with my mother.

"I need to talk to my mother in private please," I said turning to Katherine.

She was looking me dead in my eyes. She did not stop rubbing my hand. She was not leaving.

I then turned to my mother. I locked eyes with her.

"Why? I found the letters."

My mother knew I was not going to say exactly what was going on in front of Katherine. She did it for me.

"He wrote me first."

I laughed. I could not believe my mother was playing games!

"He said you wrote him first!"

"He wrote me! He asked about her."

"That made you feel it was okay for her to write him?"

"It was the right thing to do."

"I don't want her communicating with him!" I snapped. "He tried to kill me! He does not care about her! If he would have succeeded, I wouldn't be here, and neither would he! Then what? She and Braylon both would have been without both of their parents!"

"He is remorseful!"

"He is spiteful!"

"He is not!"

"He is using you to use her to get back at me! You think you know him! You don't know him! You never knew the real him."

"He is her father!"

"Matthew Franklin is her father!"

I was in her face! I was not moving! We were standing toe to toe. Eye to eye.

Katherine stepped in between us. "Calm down Brooke."

"He has done more for her than Carson ever did, and Carson lived in the same house with us! Cassidee even knows that," I yelled.

"At the end of the day Matt is not her biological father," said my mother.

She was touching a very sensitive spot. Angry was not even the word. I was more furious. Just when I thought we were working things out, she went and jumped back on the bandwagon with Carson.

Katherine and I were sitting on the swing in her backyard. I was so upset with my mother. Katherine was talking to me. She was trying to make me feel better. I was just staring into space. I was not even listening to her. That was rude. I knew that. I just could not wrap my mind around the fact that my mother was making my daughter write my ex-husband after he tried to kill me. There was only one thing on my mind.

"Don't tell Matt," I said as the tears consumed me.

Katherine sighed. "As much as I want to, I am not. I told myself that I would not get into your marriage."

"This has nothing to do with my marriage."

Katherine smiled and rubbed my face.

"It has everything to do with your marriage sweetheart."

She had my attention. I was listening then.

"It became about your marriage the day you decided not to tell him. He is your husband. When you two became one, your children became his. Even before you all were married, you knew how he felt about Cassidee and Braylon. He loves them as if they were his own. You should have told him the day you found the letters."

I shook my head no at her. I could not tell Matt. She knew how he was. I was not understanding. Matt was going to lose his mind. As much as I was angry at my mother, I loved her. She and I never had the best relationship. I was happy we had a relationship at all. If Matt found out, that would be no more. Not only would our relationship no longer exist, but my husband would also no longer trust my mother. Their relationship would not be the same. Their relationship would be ruined. I did not want them to be feuding and I would be stuck in the middle. I did not want my children in a dysfunctional family.

Chapter 4

Matt

The new location for our third location of Lady In Red was finished. James, Phayla, and I were scheduled to meet there to review the building before we started to move merchandise in. James took the day off. He still agreed to meet us there. Phayla and I left the office together. She had not been herself lately, I asked her about it while I drove to the location.

"What's going on Lil Sis?"

She rolled her eyes. "Not you too!"

"What?" I laughed.

She shook her head. "Brooke and Asia were asking me the same thing."

"You have been acting differently."

"Nothing is wrong alright."

"You know I know you're lying. The thing is, I don't know why you're lying to me. Unless a man broke your heart. Do I need to break his face?"

She laughed. "Yikes! See, that is why you would not know if I was upset with a man."

"Oh, so it is a man?"

She kept laughing. "It's not! Calm down."

"Yeah okay," I laughed.

I drove onto the newly paved parking lot. James was there. We noticed his SUV. We got out of the car and headed inside. I opened the door for Phayla, and she walked in. We heard laughter. It was a female. We then heard footsteps. James came from the back of the building. He was not alone. Phayla and I looked at one another. Then back at the female! Then back at each other again! I could not believe it.

"Hey," said James. "I brought my friend with me. I hope you all do not mind."

I eyed Roslyn. For some odd reason, Phayla was eyeing her too.

"Um, I don't mind," I said. "Phayla?"

Phayla smirked. "It's nice to see you again Ms. Roslyn."

James eyed Phayla. Phayla rolled her eyes at him.

"You two know each other?"

Roslyn smiled. "Yes. I had my first interview with Phayla."

"I see you made it to the second one with James," I said eyeing her.

Roslyn eyed me. "I did not."

I then looked at Phayla. She looked away from me and made her way toward the dressing rooms. We had a strict interview process. Candidates were to have their first face-to-face with her. Then James and I was the final stop. I was wondering why Roslyn never made it to the second phase. I was happy she did not get hired. The girl practically told me she wanted me, yet she was standing there with my right-hand man. I was still curious as to why she did not make it to the second phase. I was also curious about her feelings for James. What were her intentions?

My cell phone began to vibrate in my jacket pocket. My sister was calling.

"Hey Melissa," I answered.

"I need you to come to mama's house ASAP."

She was visiting from Vegas. I knew something was wrong!

"Is Mama okay?"

"Just get over here!"

"I am on my way!"

I then said to Phayla and James, "I have to get to my mom's place."

"Is everything okay?" asked Phayla.

"I don't know!"

I parked my car in my mother's driveway. I got out of the car and rushed to her door. I opened the door with my key. Melissa was standing in the living room. She was shaking.

"Is Mama okay?"

"She went to the store."

"Then what's wrong? Where is Madeline? Did she take her with her?"

"That's why I called."

"What's wrong?" I asked her.

Melissa started to cry. I did not need her crying. She was scaring me!

"Melissa!"

"She was sleeping. She woke up screaming. I went into the room, and I said her name. She did not turn my way. I went over and reached for her. She did not reach out to me. I was right there."

"Okay, where is she now?"

"Upstairs playing. It took her a while to respond to me. Then she just did it again. She was asking me where her toys were. They were right there Matt. I watched her for a while. She soon started to move again. That's when I called you.

I slowly sat down on the couch. I was trying to process what my sister was telling me. I did not want to believe it. I covered my face in disbelief. I heard Madeline scream out from the room. She was calling for my sister. I got up from the couch and we ran upstairs to the playroom my mother had for my children. She had fallen. We were standing at the door watching her. She was on the floor not moving.

"Madi," I said to her. "Are you okay?"

"Daddy," she said beginning to look around.

"Yeah come here," I said.

She pushed herself up from the floor. She sat there for a second and began to look around. She was looking for me.

"I'm right here baby. Come to daddy."

She stood up. She reached out for me. She wasn't moving. I looked at my sister who was already crying. I could not hold back my tears. I made my way over to my baby girl and picked her up.

"Daddy," she said to me.

I turned to Melissa who was still standing in the doorway.

"It's not all the way gone. She still can see."

"I'm going to go call Brooke. She will be here to pick her up soon."

"No," I said. "Don't. I'll handle it."

Melissa then said, "Matt, I know you. You did not want to accept for the longest that you were blind. You're not going to tell her."

"You're not either!" I snapped. "I am going to fix this before she even finds out."

"What?" she asked me.

"Don't tell mama either!"

"What are you going to do?"

"I'm going to figure it out. Just keep this between us okay!"

"Alright," cried Melissa.

Brooke

Dinner was served. The children were bathed and in bed. Matt was lying in bed when I came into our bedroom from reading Madeline a bedtime story. I pulled the covers back and got into bed with him. He cut the television off. He pulled me into his arms. He kissed me on my lips.

"I need to talk to you," he said to me.

I looked up at him. "What's going on?"

"I need to go to Vegas for a while. The company is having some issues. I need to fix some things there."

"How long?" I asked him.

"A month or two."

"Why so long?" I asked him.

Matt and I had not been apart in a long time. I was used to him flying in and out of Vegas. It had been years since he was gone for long periods.

"Well, I mean I am not going right away. I must go to a couple of meetings first. After those meetings with some partners to fix the errors, I'll need to go and stay."

I did not want to be away from Matt that long. Just as I did not want to be away from him that long, I also supported him. I did not want to seem selfish.

"I understand," I said. "I'm going to miss you of course, but I understand."

He kissed me. "Thank you for understanding. I'm going to miss you too. One more thing, can Madi come with me?"

I had to laugh. He must have been out of his mind if he thought I was going to deal with Madeline by myself for two months.

"Um yeah! I'm not dealing with the spoiled one while you're gone! When you're working is she going to be with your sisters?"

"I didn't think about that," said Matt to me. "I will talk to them. That would work!"

My phone sounded. I had a notification. I picked it up from the nightstand. There was a new email. It read instacontact:CDavis. Carson was emailing me from the prison! I did not want to open the email. I did not want Matt to see the message. I hurried and deleted it. I knew he knew my email. I knew my mother was not crazy enough to give the man my home address. I had a feeling she told him about me confronting her.

Matt

Melissa joined me and Madi on my private jet. I couldn't help but stare at my only biological child as we flew over the sky. She was sleeping so peacefully in my arms. I was worried about her. I had a hard time adjusting when I first lost my eyesight. I knew things were going to be worse for her. Mainly because she was very small. I scheduled an appointment for the same day. I used my time at work to call around to physicians in Vegas. I had to try to fix her sight before Brooke found out.

She did well with the doctor. He performed a series of eye exams. We were sitting in the doctor's office waiting for him to return with the results. Brooke called me. I answered.

"Hey, sweetheart."

"Hey," she said. "How is everything going? You didn't call me."

"I fell asleep," I lied. "I am so sorry sweetheart."

"It's fine," she said. "I understand, where is Madi?"

"She is sleeping too," I lied again.

"She did okay on the flight?" she asked me.

"Perfect," I said.

"I miss you two already," she said.

"We miss you too."

The door opened. The doctor walked in.

"Hey sweetheart, Madi is waking up. I'm going to call you back."

"Okay," she said. "Love you!"

"Love you too sweetheart," I said before ending the call.

The doctor then said, "We have good and bad news."

I knew that! I just did not want the confirmation. I lowered my head.

"She is losing her eyesight. That is why she is having periods when she can see and other times, she is unable to. She can have the surgery. It will be risky because of how small she is."

"We have to have the surgery," I said to him.

The doctor sighed. "Mr. Franklin, your file was sent over. You barely made it. I do not advise that you put your daughter's small body through that.

I watch the doctor flip through the pages of my file. He was looking for something. I could tell by the way he was concentrating.

He looked up at me and asked, "Your condition was not hereditary?"

"No," I said. "I fell from a building."

The doctor shook his head. "Her condition is hereditary."

"No one in my family is blind," I said.

"Are you sure?" he asked me.

"I'm sure," I responded.

The doctor lowered his head and repeated himself. "There is history in either your family or the mother's family."

I was sure there was no history of eyesight loss in either one of our families. The doctor was thinking just the opposite. There was only one way to find out.

My father was already living in Las Vegas. I flew my mother out. She thought it was to help my sisters with Madeline. We were to meet at my house there in Vegas. I was sitting at my dining room table waiting for them to arrive. Surprisingly, they arrived at the same time. They each sat down at the table.

"I need to tell you all something. I do not want Brooke to know right now. I thought I was going to be able to fix it. I can't. I just may have to tell her. Before I tell her, I need to have all the details."

"What do you need us to do?" asked my mother.

"I need you all, to be honest with me."

My mother and father were both confused. I watched them eye one another. My father then said,

"We're listening Son."

"Which side has a history of eyesight loss?"

Neither one of them gave me an answer. They probably thought I was referring to myself. I watched my mother lower her head.

"You're losing your sight again?"

"Mama, I don't mean any harm, I just really want to know the answer."

She did not bother to lift her head. I looked down the table at my father. He was fidgeting with his fingers. They knew! Someone was about to tell me.

"It's not me," I said. "Madi is losing her sight."

My mother immediately looked up at me.

"How do you know this?" she asked me. She was about to cry any minute.

"The doctor told me it was hereditary."

I was becoming angry! I wanted an answer and I wanted it right then and there!

"I know one of you know," I said beginning to raise my voice.

My mother started to cry.

"It's not my side," she cried.

I looked down the table again at my father.

"Is it your side?"

He would not answer me. I stood up and hit the table.

"Answer me!"

My mother rose to her feet. She begged me to calm down. There was no calming down! My daughter was losing her sight and they were not giving me answers.

"Yes," he said to me.

I turned to my mother. "Did you know any of this?"

"No," she cried.

"Don't lie to me, Mama!" I snapped.

"Don't talk to her like that!" snapped my father standing to his feet.

I slowly turned my head. He and I were staring each other dead in the eyes.

"Who are you talking to?" I asked him. "You stopped being my daddy a long time ago."

My father then said, "I made some mistakes in my past. Some toward your mother. Many toward you and your siblings. The main one was toward you. I left and I failed to come back when your mom told me you were blind. I knew then you inherited the trait from my grandmother. I couldn't face you. It was already hard enough for me to deal with the pain

I caused you all. Then to know you were blind. I ran again. I never would have imagined Madi would be losing her sight. I am so sorry."

"I don't want your apology," I snapped cutting him off. "You can get out of my house."

My father pleaded with me to stay. "I was not there for you. Don't make Madi go through this alone. I want to be there for all of you."

"Get out!" I yelled.

My mother stood up. "Just listen to him. Hear him out."

"Hear him out!" I yelled. "Let me guess, you heard him out?"

My father said to me, "I am only going to tell you one more time to stop yelling at your mother. Yes, she heard me out."

My mother said, "If I can hear him out, you can too."

I smirked. "What is this? You two are taking up for each other now! What are y'all doing? You showed up here together. Y'all must be sleeping together!"

I felt my mother's hand go across my face. The slap stung. I forgot how they felt over the years! She slapped all the taste out of my mouth. She took me back to my childhood.

She then said to me, "I get that you're upset right now, but you will not disrespect me. You remember who took care of you when he did leave! Was I mad then? Yes! Over the years, I had to forgive him! We walked in here together because I forgave him! He forgave himself! We have grandchildren we need to make things right for!"

My mother turned to walk out of my dining room. She stopped at the entranceway and turned to me,

"By the way, if I'm sleeping with your father, that's my business!"

Chapter 5

Brooke

We met our friends for a night out at a local lounge. Matt and Terry were playing a game of pool. Asia, Phayla, and I were sitting at the table. Asia and I were drinking wine. Phayla was indulging in Hennessey. She was not talking much.

The waitress came back to the table, Phayla ordered another drink. She was going on glass number four. Asia looked at me. I shrugged my shoulders.

"Phayla, girl what's going on?" asked Asia.

Phayla asked for the waitress to come back. She was coming back as the guys were headed back to the table.

"In this case, make it two more glasses," she said to the waitress.

I was trying to figure out why she needed two more glasses. I looked around. James and an unfamiliar face joined us at the table. I knew we were about to meet the young lady when James slid his arms around her waist and pulled her to him.

"Okay, I'll get that for you," said the waitress to Phayla.

"Get her what?" asked Matt. He gently pulled me out of my chair before sitting down and placing me in his lap.

"Another drink," said Phayla.

"Well two more," said Asia.

"You been drinking all night," said Terry.

"You have," said Matt. "Maybe you need to slow down."

"How many drinks have you had?" asked James.

Phayla laughed. "Why are you worried about me? You need to introduce everyone to your girlfriend."

James cleared his throat as if he was uncomfortable, "She and I are dating."

Phayla cut him off by bursting into laughter. "Dating! Boy, it's all the same!"

James ignored Phayla, "Roslyn, this is Brooke, Terry, and Asia."

He did not introduce Roslyn to Matt and Phayla, I figured she knew them.

"You work for the company?" I asked out of curiosity.

"I didn't make it past my first interview," she said.

Matt asked her, "How is the career search going for you?"

Roslyn smirked. "It's going well. I was looking forward to working with you."

Phayla smirked. "Yeah! We know!" She picked up an empty glass.

"Where is she at with my drinks!"

James then said, "You don't need any more to drink."

Phayla laughed. "Awwwwww, you care?"

I watched as James took a deep breath before letting out a sigh. His demeanor was strange.

"I've always cared," he said to Phayla.

Phayla laughed, "Boy! Bye!"

Asia eyed me before saying, "Roslyn, you better get used to Phayla and James going at it. Girl, they have the never-ending big brother and little sister feud."

Phayla laughed aloud. "Yeah! I'm glad you're still around sis! James tries to be sneaky with his women."

James laughed. "Not all. Just some. I mean they could have been like Roslyn and accepted me when they knew I was serious."

The waitress came back to the table with Phayla's drinks.

"Girl you're just in time," she said.

James then said to Matt, "Let's get our sister out of here before she gets too wasted."

"I don't need y'all to do nothing," said Phayla drinking from the glass of Hennessey.

James took Phayla by her arm. She jerked away from him. He grabbed her a second time. None of us would have expected what she did next. She picked up the glass of Hennessey and threw it in his face. Matt rushed from the seat. Terry stepped in between James and Phayla. Matt grabbed Phayla. James did not say a word. We all knew he was upset. He walked away from the table. Roslyn followed him.

"I think we should take her home," said Asia.

"I agree," I said.

"I'll drive her car," said Asia.

On our way to Phayla's house, she was sitting on the passenger side of my car. She was just talking and talking.

"How dare him! The nerve of him! I can't believe it! Then he tried to play me in front of her! Drunk! Wasted! I'm not either! Intoxicated perhaps! He knew better! Ratchets get drunk and wasted! My classy behind just may be intoxicated!"

I wanted to tell her she was way past drunk! I could not believe she allowed herself to get that way. She was not herself. We were going to talk to her once she was sober. Asia and I stayed with her that night. We made sure she got up to her room and into her bed.

We were sitting in her living room under covers on her couches watching television.

"Girl! She was a hot mess," said Asia.

"A hot mess!" I emphasized. "Something is going on."

"She's sleeping with James."

"What! No!"

"Yes! She is! You don't pay attention! They both gave it away!"

"I don't think they are."

"Well, I think they are or were."

"Why were?" I asked Asia.

Asia folded her arms and eyed me. "Girl! You just are so lost! I need you to pay attention, Brooke! You get on my nerves!"

"Tell me," I laughed. "Too much has been going on in my life with Carson for me to be paying attention to other people's problems."

"Something else happened?" she asked me.

I told her about the constant e-mails Carson was sending me. I never opened any of them. I just always read the subject box. I knew he was trying to apologize for his actions, I never opened any. I just deleted them.

"Have you told Matt?"

"Um no!" I said.

"Yeah, he's not in there with him huh," said Asia.

"Exactly," I said. "Katherine thinks I should tell him."

"At this point, I may have to agree."

"Everything is going so good though. Matt is going to flip! I just really want it all to go away."

"He'll be on your side," Asia assured me.

"He'll be on his way to the prison," I said.

"Maybe that is what Carson needs! A good visit from Matthew Franklin."

The next morning Asia and I headed up to Phayla's room. It was super early! Sis was going to have a bad hangover. We didn't care! We wanted answers. Asia pulled the covers smooth off her.

"Wake up!"

Phayla balled up and tried to pull for the covers. I laughed.

"I have them! Wake up!" said Asia again.

"Get out," said Phayla.

"Naw! We are going to stay because you need to talk," I said.

"I have a headache!"

"No duh!" said Asia. "You should be throwing up too."

"Did all that early this morning!"

Asia laughed. "Oh! So, you were throwing up like at 5:00 a.m. Sure you're not pregnant too?"

"Leave me alone!" said Phayla.

"Yeah that's not even happening," I said sitting on the bed.

Asia sat down as well. Phayla slowly sat up. It took her about five minutes. She was feeling all the liquor. She leaned against her headboard. Her eyes were very low. Her hair was everywhere. She looked like her breath was stinking. I laughed. She gave me the middle finger. I did it back!

"What?" she asked us.

Asia then said, "Brooke here seems to think different. I don't. I think you're either sleeping with James or you were at some point."

Phayla rolled her eyes. "I could have stayed asleep for this."

"Ignoring the question huh. How long has this been going on?" asked Asia.

"Nothing is going on between me and James," said Phayla.

"Told you," I said.

"Shut up!" said Asia to me. Asia then said to Phayla, "You gave it away at the restaurant. I should have recorded you! What is going on?"

"What happened at the restaurant?" asked Phayla.

Asia laughed. "James brought his new chick to the restaurant and you showed out!"

Phayla rolled her eyes. There it was! We caught her!

Asia then said, "The eye roll said it all! Tell us now!"

"I just don't like her!" said Phayla.

"Lies!" laughed Asia.

"Y'all are not going to leave me alone huh?" snapped Phayla.

"Tell us the truth and we'll leave you alone," said Asia.

Phayla rolled her eyes. "We were messing around! We aren't any more! Leave me alone!"

I was shocked! I grabbed my mouth to keep from screaming.

"I knew it!" said Asia

"Shut up!" said Phayla. "Don't make this into anything! We are done! We are over!"

I then said, "Wait a minute y'all! To be honest, I think you are hurt behind you all ending. Your actions these past months say you are hurt."

"I don't want to talk about It," she snapped.

Asia said, "All jokes aside. Girl if you need to talk, let's talk. Do not be around here drinking and being all depressed about it."

Phayla looked at me. "Just don't tell Matt okay."

I wondered what Matt had to do with the situation. I asked her. She thought she was going to get off easy by continuing to beg me not to tell him.

"I am going to ask him why you don't want him to know if you don't tell us," I said to her.

Phayla closed her eyes. Tears began to fall. Asia got up from the bed. She went into her master bathroom and came back with a tissue. Phayla took the tissue from her and wiped her face.

"He doesn't like employees to date. James was at the company first when I came. He was interested in me. It was at the time when Matt was building the company. We did not start to mess around physically until Matt was blind."

Asia smiled! "Please tell me y'all messed around in that house!"

I hit Asia. She laughed.

"Girl what? You know how big the house is in Vegas! I would have been all over it with Terry!"

"You're nasty!" I said to her.

Phayla laughed. "I needed that laugh. To answer your question, we messed around in the house but not all over the house. He would come to my side and I would go to his."

"Why did you all end things?" I asked her.

"It wasn't about us ending things," she said to us. "James wanted us to be open about things. Matt has his sight back, I know how he is going to be, I don't want to deal with him."

I then said to her, "You can't stop living because of Matt. He will be mad at first because you all snuck around in his house. I know my husband. He will get over it at the same time."

"My career," said Phayla. "I don't want to lose it."

"You won't," I said to her. "Matt loves you and James. He will be just fine."

Phayla sighed. "It's a lot more to the situation. James wants to get married. I can't."

Asia stood up from the bed. "Say what! I know I'm married, and we can even fight after I say this! To be old, James is fine! He can get all the business! He is a sweetheart! He is gentle! He asked you to marry him and you said no!"

"This is why I did not want to talk about this!" said Phayla. "It's too much for me as is. My career is just starting."

Asia rolled her eyes. "Tell that lie to somebody else. You're keeping something from us."

Chapter 6

Matt

I had to get a second opinion about Madeline's eyesight. We headed back to Las Vegas. The second doctor felt the same as the first doctor. I had to get her eyesight corrected! I could not allow Brooke to go through what she went through with me again. She was going to be devastated. I was devastated! After the visit, my sister, Madeline, and I headed back to the house. Melissa took Madeline out for a while. I needed time to myself. I decided to take a swim in my indoor pool to clear my head. I was swimming in the water and all the memories came back to me from when I was blind. I had to learn so much! I did not want Madeline to experience that. I came up from the water. I had a thought! I tried to avoid Dallas because Brooke would find out. I did not have a choice now. Maybe a doctor in Dallas could perform her surgery. My operation was a success there. I then knew I had to tell Brooke. I left Madeline with Melissa and headed back to Dallas.

The alarm sounded when I opened the front door. It was after midnight. I knew Brooke would be sleeping. I was not going to wake her. I decided to tell her in the morning. I walked quietly up our staircase. I was about to walk down the hallway when I noticed Cassidee's light was on. I stepped into the room to turn the light off. She jumped in her bed. She then began to shuffle papers in her lap.

"Hey Angel," I said to her.

"Hey Daddy," she said.

"Why are you up so late? It's time to go to bed."

"I was just drawing," she said.

"Oh really," I smiled. "Let me see," I said walking over to her.

She hid the papers and said, "No!"

Her tone was unusual. I watched her lower her head. She then started to cry. I had a feeling she was not drawing.

"You're not drawing, are you?" I asked her.

"No sir," she said crying.

"Can I see what you're doing?" I asked her.

More tears flowed and she said, "Mama said, if I told the truth, you wouldn't be mad at me."

She handed me the paper. I saw it was a letter. She was writing a letter to Carson. As much as I wanted to ball the letter up. I held my composure in front of her. My thought of what she said before handing the letter to me came back.

"Mama knows about the letters?"

"Yes sir," she cried. "Please don't be mad at me."

I kissed her on her cheek, and she hugged my neck.

"Daddy will never be mad at you. Stop crying okay."

"Okay," she said.

After soothing my angel and reading a story to her, she was sleeping. I headed to our master bedroom; Brooke was about to get up! I walked into the room and noticed she had fallen asleep with her laptop in her lap. I picked up the laptop. I noticed she was about to reply to an email. I read the subject box. It read, instacontact:CDavis. She too was writing Carson!

I decided not to wake her. My level of anger was going to wake the children. We never argued in front of them. I needed to clear my mind. I left the house. I left the state! I flew back to Las Vegas.

I let Melissa keep Madeline a little while longer. She stayed with her the next day and night. I did not tell her what I found. She was only going to be on her way to Dallas! Brooke called and called that day and night. I did not answer her. I did not want to talk to her. I made excuses as to why I could not talk. I did text her and let her know that Madeline was with Melissa if she wanted to talk to her.

That night, I found myself in a local club. I was sitting at a table having drinks alone. I heard a familiar voice. I had not heard it in a long time.

"Matthew?"

I slowly rose my head to see my ex-girlfriend standing in front of me. Nicole still looked the same. She and I dated before I lost my sight. Her light brown skin tone jogged my memory. Her natural brown hair had been straightened. It was hanging down with a middle part.

"Wow," I laughed. "Yeah, it's me."

Nicole tilted her head, "You can see me?"

I smiled, "Yes."

"Oh my God!" she said.

I stood up and hugged her.

"How have you been?" I asked her.

She was silent. She was staring at me. I knew she was still in shock that I could see.

"You're making me uncomfortable," I laughed.

"I'm so sorry," she said. "I just can't believe it."

"I had another surgery," I said to her.

She lowered her head. I thought back to where we were in our relationship when I had my first surgery.

"Don't feel bad," I said to her. "It's over and done with."

She slowly lifted her head. I sat back down in the booth.

"You can sit down."

She sat down in the booth. "I'm sorry."

I smirked and took a drink from the bottle.

"You're okay. It seems like lately, all the people around me are hurting me and I'm living with their hurt. I don't want to re-live yours. So, let's not go there."

"Okay." She sighed. "I heard you moved to Dallas. What are you doing here?"

"Had to come back for a little business."

"I do see the advertisements for the new products. Still going strong. Your construction company also did the new casino here. That's what's up!"

"Yeah," I smiled. "Thanks. What have you been up to?"

"Just working," she smiled. "I have my own business now too. I have a shoe store."

"That's good," I smiled. "Proud of you."

She smiled. "Yeah, I was always good at picking out your top sellers for your Lady in Red Bottoms Line."

I laughed. "Yeah, you were."

"Always had to compete with Phayla," she laughed. "Is she still there?"

"Still there," I laughed. "Don't start on her."

Nicole laughed. "Okay, I'll let her live. Sheesh! She didn't like me! I did not have a problem with her."

I was no longer laughing. "Phayla kind of was right."

She lowered her head again and said, "You said you didn't want to re-live that. Why bring it up?"

"You brought up Phayla."

The waitress came back to the table. I asked for another drink. Nicole then said,

"I will take a Long Island Iced-Tea."

"I hope you are paying for that," I laughed.

"No, you are," she laughed.

The more we talked, the longer we stayed. The longer we stayed, the more we talked. Drinks kept coming to the table.

Nicole downed another glass. "Let's dance."

She got up from the booth and pulled me to the dance floor. She had too much to drink. She wrapped her arms around my neck. I was still halfway sober.

"You look good," she said to me.

"Thank you. You don't look half bad yourself."

"We stayed coming here," she smiled.

"It was our spot."

"We had some good times here."

"I remember," I said eyeing her. I was trying to figure her out. I thought she was on a mission to get me back.

"I think we had more good times than bad," she said to me.

I tried to think about the good times we had. There were some. I do remember a lot of bad times.

"You did too much stuff, Nicole."

"I was a fool back then," she said to me.

"You were," I agreed.

"I was selfish."

"Very," I agreed.

"I lost a good man."

"You did."

"I'm sorry."

"I heard you earlier."

"I've missed you."

"I'm married."

Nicole moved closer to me, "So why are you here alone?"

"Just know that I am married," I said easing away from her.

She placed her arms back around my neck. I removed her arms.

"I'm serious Nicole."

Madeline and I were spending daughter daddy time together. I decided to take her to the mall. She loved to make bears at Teddy Bear World. The location was better than the one in Dallas. I just had to take her after we ate lunch.

We were walking through the mall. She was super excited.

"Daddy! We going to get bears!"

I laughed. "Say we are going to make bears."

She smiled at me. "We are going to make bears."

"That's my girl," I smiled.

She said bears! As in more than one! She was going to break me!

"You can only get one bear," I laughed.

"With clothes!"

"With clothes," I smiled.

I picked her up and tossed her in the air. She laughed and smiled. I kissed her on her cheek.

"I love you!"

"I love you, Daddy!"

I heard Nicole say, "You have a daughter?"

I put Madeline down. She grabbed me by my hand and hid behind me. I didn't say a word to Nicole. I just looked at her. She then said,

"I apologize for the other night. I had too much to drink. I was not trying to disrespect you or your marriage." She looked down at Madeline. "Your family."

I sighed. "No, let me apologize. I should not have even sat there that long and had all those drinks with you. Especially with our history."

"I mean, we ended as friends."

I tilted my head to the side. I was trying to figure out how we ended as friends. That was not how I remembered it. Instead of going back down the horrible memory lane with her. I just said,

"If that's what you want to think."

I then began to walk past her with Madeline.

"Excuse us, we have to get to Teddy Bear World."

Nicole hurried and said, "I am actually about to meet my son there."

Last I knew, she did not have any children. I did not want to get into another conversation with her. I just kept walking.

Madeline saw the sign of the store and took off running. I hurried behind her. She ran into the store. She was greeted by a teenage girl. The young lady kneeled and asked her name. She took her by her hand and they headed to build a teddy bear. Madeline knew the routine. She pulled the girl over to the bears. They started to look around. The girl turned to me.

"You must be dad?"

Madeline yelled out, "No! That's my daddy!"

We laughed. I said, "Yes, I am her daddy!"

"Are we just purchasing any bear?"

I smiled. "Let her have her way!"

The girl smiled. "Sounds like my dad! She's going to have the best life at 16! I just got my car!"

I laughed. "Don't rush her! I have another older one! They tax me all of the time."

The young girl made her way back over to Madeline. Madeline was jumping and pointing at a bear. The girl took it down for her. Madeline ran back over to me with the bear.

"Daddy! I got this one!"

I smiled. "I see!"

"Come make it with me," she said grabbing my hand.

I heard a commotion behind me. Others and I in the store turned around. Nicole and a man were standing in the entranceway of the store arguing.

"I've been here waiting on you!" yelled the man.

"I'm here now," she said. "I told you traffic was horrible."

"You should have left early! What were you doing?"

Nicole said, "You just want to find something to argue about. I'm not doing this with you. Not right here. Thank you for bringing him to me."

I knew the man. I just did not know she had a child with him. Before I could turn back to Madeline he said,

"Oh! So, you must be back with him?"

Nicole did not respond to him. She took her son by the hand. She was walking away from Edward when he grabbed her by her arm and jerked her back to him. As much as I did not want to interfere, I had to! I could not stand for any man to place his hand on a woman!

I walked over to them. "Let her go, Edward."

He laughed. "You can see now? Congratulations!"

I smirked. "Just let her go."

"Still defending the woman who doesn't want to be with you."

"We are not together," I snapped. "Now let her go!"

He would not let her go. I pushed him. He stumbled back.

"I'm glad you can see homie!" he said to me. "This ain't over."

I did not respond to him. I headed back into the store to Madeline. Nicole came rushing behind me. I sighed. I did not want to deal with her! She rushed in front of me.

"Christopher, go make you a bear," she said to him.

The small boy walked slowly over to the wall of bears to pick a bear.

"Thank you," she said to me.

"You had a baby by him?" I asked her.

She lowered her head. "I did."

"Why?" I asked her.

"You were not trying to be with me."

She had to be joking. She was not going to blame me for her mistake!

"It's my fault that you laid down with that bum?"

She folded her arms. "You know what I mean!"

People in the store were starting to stare at us! I knew we were loud. I headed to a nearby bench right outside of the store. She followed. We sat down.

"I don't know what you mean!" I snapped. "You left me for him!"

"I tried to come back to you!" she said.

I smirked. "After I told you no, you still went back to him!"

She sighed. "Matthew! I was young!"

"I knew you were young from the beginning Nicole! I knew you were stupid for leaving me! Young and stupid!"

"Just rub it in my face."

"I'm not rubbing anything in your face. I just can't believe it. Now you're stuck with him for 18 plus years."

She rolled her eyes and threw herself back on the bench.

"How long was he hitting you before you walked away?"

She got up from the bench. I hurried and grabbed her arm.

"I'm not trying to make you mad. I just want you to be careful."

"I didn't know you still cared."

"Didn't you just apologize earlier for trying to come on to me and you're doing it again?"

Nicole lowered her head. "Do you want me to apologize again?"

"No. I feel like you are going to keep doing it. Back to Edward, you know what happened to my mother. I just don't like a man hitting a woman. You also have your son who needs you. He is too young to lose you."

"Yeah I know," she said.

Madeline was standing in the entranceway of the store yelling for me. She was ready to check out. I walked back into the store. She showed me her bear.

"It's pretty!" I said. "You did a good job!"

"Thank you, Daddy!" she smiled.

Chapter 7

Brooke

Matt had not been talking to me. When I called him, he would not answer the phone. He would only text me. Melissa had Madeline a lot. I knew he was very concerned about the success of the company. He had to be stressed out. I even asked him to come to visit, he told me he was fine. I knew him. He was just telling me that because he did not want me worried about him.

The elevator door opened to the company. I headed to Phayla's office. I knocked on her door before walking in. She told me to come in.

"Hey girl!" she said turning around from her computer.

"Hey!" I smiled.

"What's up? What are you doing here?"

"I came to talk to you about the main site in Vegas."

Phayla looked confused. I sat down in the chair in front of her desk.

"What about the main company?"

"Matt said there were some issues there he had to go clear up."

Phayla still had the confused look on her face.

"Matt is there now," I said to her.

Phayla was quiet. I knew something was wrong. She picked up her phone and called James. Seconds later, he walked into the office.

"Did Matt tell you anything about the main site?" she asked him.

"Hey Brooke," he said reaching down and hugging me. "No, he didn't. What's up?"

"He told me he had to go there to fix some things," I said.

James then had a confused look on his face.

"He has been going there," I said. "This is his second trip."

James then said, "He told me the New York site."

"Same here," said Phayla.

"Something is going on," I said to them.

"Company issues," said James. "I'll handle it."

"He's stressing," I told him. "He's barely talking to me. You know how he is about this company."

Phayla picked up a piece of paper from her desk. She started to fan herself.

"We know," she said. She asked James, "You want me to call as well?"

"Just handle things here," said James. "I will call."

"Thanks. I just love you both," I said.

I stood up and hugged James. Phayla got up from her chair. She was still fanning. We hugged each other. She was on her way back to her desk when she collapsed.

Phayla

I woke up in a hospital bed. I had no idea I was there. I sat straight up. I locked eyes with James. My heart started to pound.

"What happened?" I asked him.

"You passed out in the office."

"Talking to you and Brooke."

"Yeah," said James.

"Where is she?"

"She went to pick the kids up from school. I stayed here."

My heartbeat picked up! I was nervous!

The hospital room door opened. A male doctor walked in. I recognized him. I was hoping he would not say too much in front of James.

"You work here too?"

"When they are short on staff," he smiled.

"I'm placing you on bed rest. Your blood pressure was high, and you are very fatigued. I'm glad I was here. Saved you an appointment."

I smiled at him. "Okay, thank you."

I was hoping he would hurry and leave! I did not want to discuss things in front of James! My doctor then turned to James.

"It's great to finally meet you. Phayla told me you would be at the next appointment. I hate we had to meet under these circumstances. Just know the baby is fine."

I could have passed back out! My heart fell to the bottom of my stomach.

James waited for the doctor to leave out of the room. He started to yell.

"When were you going to tell me?"

"Didn't you just hear that man say my blood pressure was high? You are not helping!"

"You're pregnant! How long have you known?"

"Long enough!" I said.

"You knew the night at the bar? You were drinking!"

"I didn't know then!" I snapped. "I found out after that!"

"Why didn't you tell me?"

"You have your little girlfriend!" I snapped.

James snapped back.

"Don't bring her into this! I'm talking about the baby you're carrying!"

"Yeah you're right," I said. "I'm carrying it! My baby!"

"My baby!" he snapped back at me.

There was nothing I could say. I was carrying his baby. I knew I was carrying his baby. There was no doubt in my mind. My baby did not belong to any other man. James was the father of my baby.

James stood up from the chair. He walked over to the side of the hospital bed.

"He put you on bed rest. You are going to be on bed rest. When I call Matt, I am going to let him know. We are going to work everything out."

I hated when James acted as though he was my father! I was grown! That was one reason why we were not together! He always wanted things his way!

"You are not my father!" I snapped.

"Just like you are not your mother!" he snapped. "As I said, we are going to work it out. End of discussion. I'll be back to get you when they discharge you."

James

I walked into my apartment. Roslyn was there. I was not expecting her to be there. She was in my kitchen cooking. She walked over to me. She wrapped her arms around my neck.

"Hey babe!" she said. "I wanted to surprise you. I'm cooking your dinner."

She leaned in to kiss me. I moved my head away from her.

"Are you okay?" she asked me.

There was so much going on. I did not know where to start. I especially did not know how to tell her Phayla was carrying my child. For some odd reason, I knew they did not like each other. I just didn't know why they did not like one another. I did not want to know. That would only add on to the pile. There was a reason why Matt was not telling us about the issues going on with the company. The company that Phayla and I helped him build. I was not ready for that. I needed to get my mind together. Everything else was hindering me from that!

I sat down on my couch. She sat next to me. She rubbed her hand down my chest.

"You want to talk about it?"

"It's so much," I said to her. "Some issues are going on with one of our sites. Matt did not tell us."

"You're upset about it?"

"If anything is going on, he should have told us. It's just the principle. Normally, he would let us know."

Rosalyn then said to me, "I need to tell you something. It's about Matt."

I immediately turned to her. I wanted to know what she had to tell me.

"I'm just putting everything together," she said. "I did not get hired. We start to date and now he is not telling you things about the company."

"What are you saying?" I asked her.

"I did not interview with Phayla or you. I interviewed with him. During the interview. He made a pass at me. I declined it."

She was making sense. I got up from the couch. I stormed into my bedroom. I went to my closet. I took out my suitcase. I began to toss clothes in it.

"What are you doing? Where are you going?" she asked me.

"To Las Vegas."

My flight landed. I wanted to go straight to his house. I was ready to rip his head from his shoulders! I rented a car and headed to his house. I turned onto the street leading to the house. I was getting close to the gate. There was an unfamiliar car in the driveway. I then saw a woman coming out of the front door. He was with her. I recognized the woman. It was his ex-girlfriend, Nicole! I watched the two embrace. I then knew why he was there.

I was about to drive off when another car pulled behind me. The black car then sped around the rental I was driving. The window came down. A hand with a gun appeared. Shots were fired! Matt covered Nicole and they fell to the ground. The car then sped away. I was able to get the plate number. I drove up to the gate and put in the code. The gate opened and I sped up the driveway! I got out of the car and rushed up the driveway. Matt was holding Nicole in his arms. She had been shot in her back. I took out my phone and called for help.

The ambulance arrived to take Nicole to the hospital. I stood there as they placed Nicole in the ambulance. Matt was about to go with her.

"Are you coming man?" he asked me.

I could not believe he was asking me that.

"No," I said.

Melissa was running up the driveway with Madeline as the ambulance was leaving.

"Is Matt okay? What happened?" she asked me.

"Someone came by and fired shots. Nicole was shot."

"Nicole!" said Melissa. "His ex-girlfriend?"

"Yeah."

"What was she doing here?"

"I don't know," I said.

Brooke

Cassidee and Braylon were out with Katherine. Phayla and Asia were in my living room. I walked back into the living room with three glasses of wine. I handed a glass to Asia. I handed a glass to Phayla.

"No thank you," she said to me.

"Okay," I said. "Do you want anything else?"

"Water," she said.

I headed back to the kitchen to get the water. I heard my doorbell ringing. I knew one of them would answer it. I took a glass from the cabinet. I filled it with ice. I took a bottle of water from the fridge. I closed the fridge. I went back into the living room. James and Rosalyn were there. I gave the glass and water to Phayla.

"Hey," I said.

"I need to talk to you," said James to me.

I immediately thought about Matt. I became scared.

"What happened to Matt?" I asked him.

"We need to talk in private."

"You can say it in front of them," I said.

"I just really want to talk to you in private."

James insisted that we talked in private. I was not going to fight him on it. We were walking to the den when I heard my front door opening. Matt came in. I was so happy to see him. I thought something was wrong! Before I could even hug him, James said,

"You want to tell Brooke what's going on or do you want to see me first?"

I watched as Matt became uneasy. He looked confused.

"Don't give me that look," snapped James. "Tell her."

Matt then said, "I don't know what you're talking about. Brooke, I do need to talk to you."

"If you need to talk to her, you do know what I'm talking about," snapped James.

"James, please!" said Matt. "I know where you are going with this! You don't know what you're talking about!"

James did not let up.

"Which one do you want to tell Brooke first? The pass you made at Roslyn or the fact that you were seeing your ex in Las Vegas! You were not there for the company!"

I didn't know whether to punch Matt in his face or throw up on my living room floor. I was stuck. I could not move.

Phayla stood up from the couch.

"I know for a fact he did not make a pass at Roslyn! I hope to God you were not seeing Nicole's trifling behind!"

Matt said to me, "I did not make a pass at Roslyn. I was not seeing Nicole! We do need to talk about something else!"

"You weren't in Vegas for the company! I pulled up to the gate. They both came out of the house!" yelled James.

"Matt! Come on bro!" said Phayla!

"I was not seeing Nicole."

Matt turned to me. "The only person I owe an explanation to is you."

James kept going! "Don't try and take her and lie to her! Don't forget I know you! I knew you before you lost your sight! You were humble when you lost it! You got it back and you don't know how to act with the women!"

I couldn't help but think the same thing.

"That's what I was afraid of," I said.

Matt was becoming angry. I could tell! He tried to remain calm, but he couldn't keep it together.

"The dirt on my shoes means more to me than Nicole!" He then pointed at Roslyn, "This! I ain't make no pass at that hoe!"

James rushed Matt. Matt pushed him back.

"What is going on in here?" yelled Katherine.

Matt's father then stood in between Matt and James.

"Ask your son!" said James.

Katherine eyed Matt. Matt looked away.

"Mama don't start. I was here to tell Brooke everything. He brings up Nicole and Roslyn. He doesn't even know what he is talking about!"

James said, "You lied and told Brooke you were going to Vegas for the company! Nothing is wrong with the company! You tried to get with Roslyn and when I went to Vegas to confront him, he was coming out of the house with Nicole, and then a drive-by happened and he ran to the hospital with her!"

"So, there's more!" I said. "Shooting! With my baby there!"

"She was with Melissa!" said Matt. "Can we please go talk?"

Phayla then said, "Wait, James! Did you go to Vegas to confront him? Confront him about Roslyn! Sounds like you were upset about it! I knew you were full of crap at the hospital. I'm just going to do what I got to do."

Phayla grabbed her purse. She was leaving our house. James grabbed her by her arm.

"What are you trying to say?"

Phayla snatched away from him.

"You know exactly what I'm saying!"

James moved closer to Phayla. They were practically close enough to kiss. He was blowing steam! She was not backing down!

"That's our sister bro!' said Matt. "Roslyn over here got you tripping! Get out of her face!"

Phayla then said, "Yeah she does have you tripping. She's lying to you! Matt did not make a pass at her."

"Mind your business!" said Roslyn.

Phayla began to charge at Roslyn. "My brother is my business! My sister is my business!"

James pulled her back, "Just like you're my business!"

Phayla snatched away from James a second time!

"Will you make up your mind!"

James lowered his head. "I'm going to take care of my child."

Phayla smirked. "Take care of your child and be with her? You can be with anybody else for all I care, but you will not have my child around her."

Phayla then said to me, "Brooke, Matt did not make a pass at her. She probably made the pass at him!"

"She did," said Matt. "During her interview with me! Which is why she did not get hired!"

Phayla shook her head. "After my interview with her. I was late for another appointment. The elevator was taking too long. I took the stairs. I was coming out of the staircase door when I heard her on the phone on the first floor. She had other intentions. Matt and money!"

"That is why you did not want me to interview her," said Matt.

"Right," said Phayla. She then turned to James. "I guess that is when she went after you!"

Roslyn said to James. "I can explain."

Katherine stepped in. "No, you've caused enough problems. You should leave. I'm telling you to leave."

Roslyn was not moving. It was my turn!

"My mother-in-law told you to leave. I'm ready to put you out."

Asia came and stood by me. "Sis, we ain't pregnant! Get out or get put out on your face!"

Roslyn snatched her purse from the couch and left out of my front door.

Katherine turned to Matt.

"Go straighten out things with your wife!"

She turned to James and Phayla.

"You two need to figure things out. A child is now involved! Either you're going to make it work or separate and make it work! They have a guest bedroom! I'm calling the shots today! Go in there and you better come out with a solution!"

Chapter 8

Matt

Brooke and I walked into our bedroom. I sat down on the bed. I asked her to sit.

"No," she said. "I want you to talk."

I did not know where to start. I did not want to tell her about Madeline. I no longer had a choice. I did not want her to be hurt. I guess I was taking too long. She asked me a question.

"Who is Nicole?"

"My ex," I said.

"You went to Vegas to see her?"

"No," I said.

"Then why were you there?"

"I will tell you; I just need you to sit."

"I'm not sitting down," snapped Brooke. "You lied to me! You said you went to Vegas for the company! You end up there with your ex! She was in the house!"

"Nothing happened!" I snapped.

"You lied to me!"

I started to tell her about the night at the club. I then thought back to why I was at the club.

"You say I lied to you. Is lying better than not telling someone something at all?"

"What?" she snapped.

"Answer my question," I snapped.

"What are you talking about?"

"Since we're talking about exes, you knew Cassidee was writing Carson! Not only that, I came home early. You were sleeping with your laptop in your lap! He had been sending you emails! You were writing him back!"

"That gave you the okay to cheat?"

"I was not cheating on you!" I yelled.

"Then what was it?"

"No! You are going to answer my question!"

There was a knock on our bedroom door.

"Who is it?" I yelled.

My mother opened the door.

"Melissa called. Madeline had another episode."

"What?" asked Brooke. "What is wrong with Madeline?"

My mother yelled at me. "You still have not told her!"

Brooke yelled! "Tell me what? You know?"

My mother sighed. "It's not for me to tell you. Remember our conversation about Cassidee."

"I'm not talking to him!" snapped Brooke.

I turned to my mother. "You knew about Cassidee writing Carson?

"What is wrong with Madeline?" yelled Brooke.

"I got it, Mama," I said.

My mother eased away from the door. I closed the door behind her.

"I need you to sit down," I said to Brooke.

Brooke tried to rush past me to get out of the door. I pulled her into my arms. She fought and fought. She could not get from my grasp.

"Stop it and listen to me!"

She kept fighting me. I did not want to tell her at that moment. Not like that! I had no choice. She was being so combative.

"Madeline is losing her sight!"

Brooke stopped fighting me. She looked up at me. I looked down at her. Before I knew it, tears were falling from my eyes. Her eyes filled with tears. She pulled away from me. I was too weak to hold on. She sat down on the bed. The tears that were building then fell.

"That's why I went to Vegas. I was trying to get her help and her sight fixed before you found out. None of the doctors there can help her."

"Our daughter is losing her sight and you were cheating?" she cried.

"I was not cheating," I cried. "However, I need to tell you something else."

"About your ex?"

"Yes."

"I don't want to hear it! Where is my child? My child is losing her sight and you kept that from me!"

"I was thinking about us all! I get no credit for that?"

"You didn't tell me!"

"You didn't tell me about Cassidee writing Carson! You were writing him too!"

"It wasn't what you are thinking!"

"I'm saying the same thing about Nicole! You don't want to hear it!"

"I don't care about your ex!" snapped Brooke. "You should have told me about Madeline! I have to deal with it too!"

"I was trying to fix it for her!"

"You should have told me!"

"I was thinking about all of us!"

"You should have told me!"

"You don't know what it's like to be blind Brooke!" I yelled.

James

Phayla and I stood in the guest room at our friends' home. She was crying. I reached over to wipe her tears. To my surprise, she did not move. I knew I could wrap my arms around her. I did just that. She fell into my arms. I kissed her forehead. I knew she was scared.

"I was going to end things with her the day I found out you were pregnant."

"You were?" she asked me.

"Yes! You know how I feel about you. She was at my place. I was so angry with you for not telling me at the same time. I was just angry. Then when she told me about Matt, I was not mad about it being her. I thought he was messing around on Brooke. She doesn't deserve that."

"I'm so scared," she cried.

"Phayla, you are not your mother. I am not your father. Our child will not be you."

I knew why Phayla was afraid to pursue things with me. Her career was not the only thing she was afraid of losing. She was afraid of losing herself. She was much like her mother. Her mother was career-driven. Her father was much like me. He was a lot older than her mother. When they met, they hit it off! Just as Phayla and I did. The chemistry was there. The chemistry turned into love. Her father wanted things her mother was not ready for. The two married. They were not married long. The maturity levels caused much friction. Phayla was a lot more mature than her mother was at her age. She just didn't realize it because she was too afraid, she would be her mother.

Her family was from Dallas. Her parents were constantly separated. She was going from house to house. All they did was argue and fight. She felt alone. She was left in the dark due to their constant feuding. She was so mature at a young age that she wanted to enhance her career in fashion. She moved to Las Vegas to interview with Matt. She practically walked into the office and told him she was the best and only option for the job. She wasn't lying. Many of her designs and financial skills sent the company to new heights. She and Matt bonded like younger sister and brother. We too were like that at first. We soon learned we were attracted to one another. We both knew Matt would not have it. We snuck around before he lost his sight and after he lost it. He regained his sight. He found Brooke. He was happy. I wanted to be happy. I wanted to be happy with the one woman I loved. That woman was Phayla.

Phayla sat down on the bed. I sat next to her. I lifted her chin.

"Let me handle Matt. You won't lose your career."

"Okay," she said wiping her tears.

"I also need you to let me be your man. I'm not your father. I'm not trying to control you. I am not trying to tell you to stay at home and not work. You can work, be a wife, and be a mother. Will it be hard? Yes! You won't have to do it by yourself."

"Okay," she said.

I placed my hand on her stomach. She placed her hand on my hand.

"You're worried! I should be the one worried! I'm going to be an old man with a baby."

We both shared a laugh.

"I got to get back in the gym!"

She lowered her head. "I want to apologize for what I said in the living room. I wasn't going to do that. I was just angry."

"I know your heart. Abortion is not in it."

I lifted her chin. "See, you're already making mature efforts."

Phayla smiled at me.

"I love you," I said to her.

"I love you too," she said to me.

We shared a kiss.

Asia burst into the bedroom.

"Um! Please have baby number 1 first before y'all start on number 2!"

We unlocked our lips. Phayla fell into my chest laughing. I wrapped my arms around her as I laughed.

"Glad y'all made up!" said Asia. "I hate to interrupt. We need to get downstairs."

Brooke

I was sitting on my living room couch surrounding my friends and family. I did not know how to feel. I did know one thing. I just wanted to get to my baby. I did not want to talk about anything. I just wanted Madeline in my arms.

"The devil has been busy," said Katherine to all of us. "You all have decisions to make. Matt and Brooke, Madeline needs you both. She won't be able to make it through this without you all being on one accord. Trust me! I know! Matt you know! You barely made it without me and your father being together. James and Phayla, you all must stay on one accord. Don't allow your child to come into a world of friction. That Roslyn girl, you all need to stay away from her. The devil sent her into your lives. Don't let him ruin what you all have worked for and deserve."

We heard the front door open. Melissa walked in with Madeline.

"Hey, Baby!" I said reaching out for her. Madeline did not come to me. She began to look around as if she was trying to follow my voice. Melissa stormed back out of the house in tears. I then knew why she called Katherine when Matt and I were discussing things. My baby's sight was completely gone.

I wanted to be strong. I could not be. I held my mouth so she would not hear me crying. I turned to leave out of the room when Madeline said,

"Mama!"

I stopped. I turned around to see her walking toward me. I only thought back to when I used to help her father find me. I stood still and said,

"Yeah, it's me. Hey pretty girl."

She smiled and continued to walk toward me. I met her halfway and picked her up. She hugged my neck. I squeezed her tight.

Matt

I asked my mother to keep the children for us that night. Brooke and I had not discussed everything. There was no way she and I were going to be on one accord without fully discussing everything. My mother did not have a problem with it.

I dropped the kids off at her house. I returned home. Brooke was not in the living room. I went into the dining room area. She was not there. The kitchen was empty. I headed upstairs to our bedroom. Just as I was passing the patio door in the hallway, I saw her sitting outside on our deck. I opened the patio door and joined her.

"Hey," I said sitting down.

She did not respond to me.

I rubbed her leg; she did not move.

"I didn't want you to find out like that," I said to her.

"I was going to find out either way," she said.

"I just wanted it to be easier on you."

"Before we even thought about children, you told me it wasn't hereditary."

I explained to her my father was not truthful about his side of the family. She could not believe what I was saying.

"I'm sorry," she cried.

"I'm going to be okay. I hate this for Madeline." I said.

"It can be fixed right?" she asked me. "Yours was fixed."

"They are saying she's too young."

"No!" said Brooke standing up. "She's not!"

Brooke began to cry and pace. I got up from the chair and took her into my arms.

"It's all too much!" she screamed out. "What are we going to do?"

I then said to her, "We first need to put everything on the table."

"I agree," she said wiping her tears.

"What is going on with you writing Carson?"

Brooke's tears started again. She did not want to tell me. She was afraid of how I would react.

"Do you want to be with him?" I asked her.

"What?" she snapped.

"I mean you can't tell me what's going on." I walked to the edge of the deck and looked up into the night sky.

"I've dealt with this before," I said. "Nicole did the same thing. Had a good man! She wanted the one who wasn't any good. The same thing happened with her that happened to you. Letting a man put his hands on her! Now, she is in the hospital fighting for her life with a son that could be mine."

Brooke walked over to me and pushed me.

"Don't you ever in your life compare me to any other woman! That's number 1! Number 2, Carson can rot in prison and then in hell as far as I am concerned! Number 3, weren't you already with Nicole at the hospital before you came home? How about you go back!"

I didn't try to stop her. I let her open the patio door and walk inside the house. It wasn't long before I heard her car speed out of the driveway and down the street.

Chapter 9

Matt

My parents separated when I was young. I didn't believe in that. Brooke and I were not talking to one another, but I was not leaving. She was my wife. I loved her. I loved our children. I loved our family. The kids did not have to adjust to us arguing or being distant around them. We chose to keep our composure around them. They were only getting adjusted to living life with their blind younger sister. Not only were they adjusting. Brooke was as well. She was not handling it well. She was maintaining. She was trying. Her effort made me think about when we first started dating. She was afraid. She had that same fear on her face. The will was in her heart.

When the kids were away, she allowed her frustration and hurt to show. I would catch her out on the deck or in our bed crying. She would not allow me to soothe her. She would either leave out of the room or move away from me. I couldn't force her to let me be there for her. I had to wait until she was ready. That was very hard for me to do. That was not in my nature.

Brooke's mother, Naomi, and I would alternate picking the children up from school. Brooke told me she was no longer picking the children up from school. I didn't want to ask questions. I was just happy Brooke was saying anything to me at all.

I first picked up Cassidee and Braylon. My mother was babysitting Madeline. We allowed her to be with her to teach her how to live with her disability. Not only did my mother teach Madeline, but she also taught Brooke as well.

I called my mother to tell her I was on my way. She asked could she bring Madeline home. She was working with her on how to follow voices. I told her that was fine.

We arrived home. Brooke was not home. I figured she was still at work or on her way from work. Braylon ran upstairs to his room. Cassidee went and sat down on the living room couch. She folded her arms and began to swing her feet. Something was on her mind. I sat down next to her.

"What's bothering you, Angel?" I asked her.

"Grandma said that I should write my father. I didn't want to write him. I told Mama that. Mama said I don't have to write him. She told me I didn't have to worry about Grandma making me write him anymore because we were not going back over there. I just hope Grandma isn't mad at me. I don't like when people are mad at me."

I picked her up and placed her in my lap. She laid her head on my chest.

"Listen, Angel," I said. "As you grow older, people are not going to like you. They are not going to like what you want to do. That is called decision-making. You decided to tell Mama how you felt. That is okay. You should always tell people how you feel. Never be afraid to tell a person how you feel about things. People are going to get mad at you for feeling different. If grandma is mad at you, don't you worry about it."

"Okay," she said.

"You just call Daddy and I'll be right there to fix it."

After talking to my angel, I knew I had a couple of visits to make. The next day, I made my first visit. I walked into a door that led to a rather small hallway. In front of me were windows. I was instructed to go down to the last window. I did that. I sat down. It was not long before Carson was sitting down in a chair on the other side of the window. I had a lot I wanted to say to him. I gathered my thoughts before I took the phone from the hook. He took the phone from the hook.

"Well," he said. "If it isn't the famous Matthew Franklin. The big shot with the construction company and multi-million fashion company who just so happens to be playing house with my family."

I smirked. "You must have been dying to find out who I was. You either did your research or saw me make the family you once had permanently mine live on national television?"

Carson leaned back in the chair. "Neither, but Brooke has been here. She must have sent you."

I did not get comfortable. I needed him to know this was not a game. I moved closer to the window.

"She did not send me. I came on my own. Real men don't have to be told anything. If I had found out first that you were writing my daughter, I would have beat her to it."

"Your daughter!" he laughed. "Cassidee will always be my daughter and don't you ever forget it."

I smirked at his comment. He thought he was getting under my skin. He just didn't know that I knew I was getting under his.

"You're her father. She calls me daddy, there's a difference. A big difference. It's kind of sad when a child understands that. You were not a father to her when you were free and you're for sure not a father behind these bars."

"Brooke told you that huh"

"Your actions told me that! You call yourself a father! You wanted to end the life of your child's mother. You wanted to take the other parent from her. That is not a father."

"I know what I did. I don't need any counseling from you. What are you here for? To tell me to stop writing my daughter?"

I intended to tell him not to write Cassidee or Brooke. That changed on my way there. I wanted him to know that I was aware of it. I wanted him to know that I supported my wife. I wanted him to know that Brooke did not have to fight him alone.

"I'm here because Brooke, Cassidee, and Braylon are top on my priority list. You hurt them before, and I won't allow you or any person to hurt them again. Cassidee wanted a relationship with you. As she grows older, she asks questions about you. Why did dad try to hurt mama or how long does he have to be in prison? We answer her questions truthfully. You may not want to hear that. It's the truth."

Every man had a soft spot. Cassidee may not have been Carson's when he was a free man. She was his now that he was in prison. He was breaking down the more I talked about her.

"Has she ever asked to come to see me? Would you all keep her from coming?"

I said to him, "I'm still trying to work on forgiving you for taking the life of my unborn child and trying to take the life of the woman I love. Even though I'm angry and glad that you are serving time for it. I would never keep your child from you. Brooke would not either. Cassidee just has not asked to come to see you. She probably would come on her own when she is older. I sense that by the way, she asks questions. She is smart. She knows a piece of her life is missing."

Carson then said to me, "I didn't realize Brooke was pregnant until the trial. I was just so angry and filled with hatred toward her. I know it's not going to change anything. I just want to say I am sorry."

I didn't crack a smile. I did not budge. I wanted him to know I was a real man. I had a feeling he feared a real man.

"I told you I'm working on that part."

"I know man," he said to me. "I just wanted to tell you that."

I had a question for him. "What made you hate Brooke so much? She is the constant light to my darkness."

Carson sighed. "I had my demons. Still dealing with them now. Anger issues with drugs, my insecurities, and a beautiful woman that every man wanted. It didn't go too well."

"So, you would put your hands on her?"

"Till she was a bloody mess. I figured if she was beaten up, no man would want to look at her."

I didn't want to think about Brooke being beaten until she was bloody. I erased the image from my mind.

I changed the subject. "If Cassidee ever asks to see you, we will bring her. If she asks to write you, we will allow her to. Naomi does not control my household. I do. Do not write Brooke anymore."

"Respect," he said to me. "You came up here like a man. I can't do nothing but respect that."

I stood outside of the home. I pressed the doorbell. The door opened. Naomi, Brooke's mother was standing on the other side. She did not ask me to come in. It didn't matter. I did not want to go inside. There was no need for me beat around the bush.

"If my daughter ever comes back to see you, I would appreciate it if you did not make her write Carson."

"He is her father," she snapped.

"He helped create her. He hasn't done anything for her. I've done it all. She's my daughter."

Naomi then said, "Save me the speech! I had enough from Brooke!"

"Speaking of Brooke," I said to her. "Your relationship was better. You knew she was trying to have the relationship she did not have with you as a child. She even helped you move here because she wanted that relationship so bad. Now you've messed it up."

"Are you done?" she snapped.

I shook my head. I had nothing more to say.

I was working from home since the change with my family. I had not been to the company. I took a trip to the office. I knocked on the office door belonging to James. He told me to come in. I walked into his office. He turned around in his chair. We were just looking at one another. There was a second knock on his door. Phayla walked in. Her stomach was visible. I had not been visiting anyone. I had not spoken to them in a while.

"Wow," I said to her.

"I know right," she smiled. "I can come back later," she said to us.

"As a matter of fact, stay baby."

I watched as Phayla sighed. James got up from his desk. We both helped her sit down in the chair in front of his desk.

She laughed. "I'm not that big yet y'all! Calm down!"

We laughed. James then said to me, "I just want to first apologize for making assumptions about Nicole and Roslyn. I never would want to cause problems in your marriage."

"You're good man," I said.

James then said, "We also want to apologize for sneaking around behind your back when you were blind."

I had a feeling that was coming. I couldn't even be mad at him. He was being honest. Phayla then apologized as well. I accepted their apologies.

"Phayla and I are going to be together," he said to me.

I wanted them to be happy. I knew why he said that to me. They both knew I did not like employees to date. I felt it was bad for business.

"You two are not just employees," I said to them. "You are family. My right hands. I'm happy to see you two together. I'm glad. I'm ready for my niece or nephew too."

I reached out my hand to do our signature handshake with James. He accepted and we embraced.

"My guy," he said.

"My guy," I said shaking his hand.

Phayla was smiling big. I leaned down and kissed her on her cheek. "Love you, Little Sis."

"Love you too," she smiled. "Thank you."

"You're in good hands! I'm going to catch y'all later."

I was walking out of the office when James asked me, "Wait, man. How is Brooke? How are you all doing?"

I sighed. "Not good. But we're going to be okay. She thinks I cheated with Nicole. I did not. I'm just waiting on the DNA test."

"DNA test?" asked Phayla.

I placed my hands into my pockets. "She has an eight-year-old son."

"She was going between you and Edward," said Phayla, remembering when Nicole and I were dating.

"Exactly," I said.

"You already took the test."

"I did," I said. "I flew out and flew right back in. Brooke isn't talking to me. She hasn't been. It was no problem. I decided to get it over with so nothing would be in the way when she does come around."

"I think I have an idea," said James.

Chapter 10

Brooke

I walked into the Norway Airline Office from training new employees. Todd was sitting behind his desk.

He said to me, "Someone is here to see you. They are waiting for you in Latte Express."

"What?" I asked him.

"Just go!" said Todd

"Is it a new employee who got lost or something?"

"Go to Latte Express Brooke."

I rolled my eyes at Todd. I headed to the coffee shop. I walked in. I saw James was coming my way.

"You're Brooke," he said to me.

I eyed him. "What James?"

He repeated himself, "You're Brooke."

"Yeah," I said folding my arms.

"My boss would like to speak with you. If you don't mind," he said to me.

He moved to the side. Matt was sitting at a table. I then knew what the two were up to. They were reenacting the first day we met! I smiled and walked over to the table. I sat down with Matt.

"I smell the perfume you are wearing. A nice fragrance it is," he said to me.

"Thank you," I said.

"You're welcome," he said. "Brooke, is it?"

"Mrs. Brooke Franklin," I said to him.

Matt licked lips, "Now Ms. Brooke, can you stick to the script?"

I laughed. He called me Ms. Brooke when we were dating. Now that we were married, he called me that to keep things spicy.

He then said, "I know you're wondering why I wanted to speak with you. I am a very blunt individual. So, I am going to tell you exactly why I left the office, consulted with your supervisor, asked him could I meet with you, just to speak with you."

He was doing good with the reenactment. He rescheduled his flight the first time we met! I was loving it. I listened as he continued.

"Four years ago, you checked me and my assistant in. Your voice caught my attention. It has had my attention since that day. You were right. You don't compare to any other woman. I am sorry for saying that to you. Nicole can't compete with your heart. You tried with me when I was blind. Look at where we are. She left me because I was blind. She said it was too much. I did not cheat on you with her. The day James saw us hugging, she was happy that I was willing to take a DNA test. I'm willing to do whatever you want me to do to prove it."

I told him I believed him. He did not have to prove himself to me.

"I went to see Carson," he said to me.

I understood his reasoning. I respected him for that as my husband and as the father of our children.

I took out my phone. I opened my email and slid my phone across the table. The email was a message I replied to months before from Carson. In the email, I informed him to not email me. I told him I was married and loved my husband and my family. I asked that he not write Cassidee until she was fully capable and ready to make her own decisions.

Matt handed me my phone back. "I knew your heart baby. I'm sorry for that too."

"I apologize for not telling you he was writing us. I just know how you are about the kids. I know you don't play about me either. From now on, no matter what, I will communicate better."

"I will as well," he said to me. "I couldn't handle that Madeline was losing her sight. I felt it was my fault. I feel responsible now."

I had to let him know he couldn't feel that way. It was not his fault that she lost her sight. I was curious about the child who could have been his.

"The results went to the Vegas house. I didn't want Nicole having our address," he said reaching into his jacket pocket and pulling them out. "I felt you would ask. I had Melissa send them to me."

He gave the results to me. I unfolded the piece of paper and began to read it. I read it twice to make sure I was reading it correctly. The test was 99.9% accurate. Matt was not the father. I was relieved. I was also sad. Nicole's son would grow up just as Cassidee was. His father would be in prison for the rest of his life.

"I don't know what to say," I said.

Matt said to me, "It's okay to be fine with the results. I'm happy with them. I didn't want to deal with Nicole. I feel sorry for her son."

He reached across the table for my hands. I placed my hands into his.

"Now, we kind of got off the script," he said. "I would love to take you to lunch."

I laughed thinking about our first lunch date.

"I will go to lunch with you."

"You like seafood?"

"Love it," I said.

Matt got up from the table. He walked over to me and pulled me into his arms. He kissed me. I rested my hands on his chest as I shared the kiss with him.

"Okay Ms. Brooke," he said unlocking lips with me. "We gone have to make lunch real short."

"You're a mess!" I laughed.

Matt

My wife and I were back on good terms. We had one solution to our problems. We needed to communicate things to one another. Regardless of how each of us thought we would feel. Not only were we not communicating effectively, I knew the devil was trying to ruin what we had. The marriage was going great and he was not happy. He threw all kinds of stones our way. He wanted us to fail. He sent my ex back into our lives. He tried to use Carson. He even tried to act through a stranger none of us knew.

My best friends were under attack. My mother, my father, my mother-in-law, and even my children! We had some serious work to do.

I invited everyone over to our home. They agreed to come. I asked the women to prepare dinner. I left it up to them what to prepare. They said they had it under control. While they prepared dinner, I had a plan for the men. We were in our dining room area making a list of things we needed to handle as men for our women.

The ladies did a good job with the dinner. The pot roast with various vegetables and rolls was delicious! My mother did a great job as always with the peach cobbler. After dinner, we all made our way to the living room. James and Phayla sat next to one another. Terry and Asia were together. My mother and father were there. They were not seated together. Naomi was not there. I was hoping she would come. Brooke was sitting in a love seat chair. I was standing in front of them all.

"Thank you all for coming. I know that we are having a great time so far. I want us to do these types of things more often. We must stay united. We are all a family. One unit. The devil tried to pull all of us apart. We were under attack. He caught us slipping. That is okay. We all will fall short. We all know how to pull it back together. I just don't want us to go to God in times of trouble. I want us to be able to go to him at any time. More during the good times, and not just during the bad times. So, when we have these types of family gatherings, I want us to end with a prayer. The prayer right now should be a prayer of thanksgiving because we made it through everything.

We should also pray for forgiveness because we fell short."

I watched as Terry grabbed Asia's hand. She held on to his. My father went to sit with my mother. James moved closer to Phayla. Brooke joined me and took my hand.

"I agree with my husband," she said. "I had no idea he was planning this. I can say that it is well needed, and I know we are going to need it in the future. We are always going to face challenges. We should get in the habit of asking God to guide and lead us before things get rough. We should ask him to fix all issues, problems, or situations we can't see."

"Can we all join hands?" I asked them.

Each one of them joined hands until we made a circle.

"I would like for each of us to pray. I will start. I am going to ask that someone picks up when I finish until we all have prayed. We can pray for ourselves, each other, or whatever is on your heart."

We lowered our heads and closed our eyes.

I prayed for myself. I asked God to lead me to the light of forgiveness. I needed to forgive Carson. Just as I needed to forgive him, I prayed for him. I asked God to send him peace. He was worried his actions ruined his relationship with Cassidee. Even if his actions did or did not tarnish their relationship, he needed peace. He was suffering consequences for his mistakes, but I did not wish any harm to come to him.

Madeline was next on my list. She was performing well without her sight. I knew as she grew older, things were going to get harder. Cassidee and Braylon were next. My angel was so confused and needed a sense of direction. She was a child struggling with a split family. We were teaching her how to pray. Until she fully understood, her mother and I were her prayer warriors. Braylon would soon grow into a young man. I asked God to give me all the necessary abilities and skills to raise a son who was not biologically mine. I knew he would have questions. I asked God to guide my tongue.

I squeezed my wife's hand as I began to pray for her. I felt her teardrops fall onto my hand. This was not the first time I prayed for her or with her. It was a time where we had not prayed in a long time. That was our problem. Now that we were at the solution, I prayed for a sense of yearning for God's healing. I knew we would need him to heal our daughter. We could not heal her. Doctors could not heal her.

Brooke

My husband said "Amen." I picked up the prayer after him. I felt like I was starting over in my life. I knew I wasn't. That is just how I felt. I knew the feeling was not of God. I needed him to help me remove the negative spirit. I was so hurt. I did not realize the blessings I had. I only saw that Madeline was blind. I asked God to forgive me for being selfish. He had blessed me. I was thankful to him for just the presence of my daughter. I thanked him for the presence of my family.

I needed the demon of fear to be rebuked. I was still fearful after 4 years of God showing me, I had nothing to be fearful of. I knew that was only the devil. I knew better. My mind became clouded again and I allowed the fear to re-enter my heart. I was fearful I would lose my mother if I told Matt she was the reason why Cassidee was writing Carson. God reminded me I only needed him. He showed me that I could not risk the blessings he had for me for a person who may not want to receive me as their blessing. Matt was that blessing. God gave me my husband not for me to risk him for my mother. He was first in my life now. I was afraid to lose him for a person who never made me first in her life.

I prayed for my mother as well. She had not been the best mother to me. I knew she wanted to be there for my children. I prayed that God showed her how to be there for them the correct way.

Phayla

It was my turn. I had not prayed in so long. I just allowed everything to pour out. I needed to get it all out. There was no better way to let it out than to give it all to God. I needed to be freed of a statistical mind. Just because my mom was a statistic did not mean I would be one. She was not the best mother and wife, that did not mean I was going to follow in her footsteps.

My health was not the best. I worried too much. I could not worry while carrying a baby. I gave all my burdens over to God. I too had a guilty heart. I asked him to forgive me for not trusting him and trusting in men the wrong way. I no longer wanted to use James as just a person to help me get through tough times or be that fix for me whenever I needed him. I decided to accept his presence in my life the way God saw fit.

James

I was not a man of tears. By the time the prayers made their way around to me, I was in tears. Mainly my tears were tears of joy. It was good to see my family praying together. It was a weight lifted from me before it was my turn. I knew that if they were praying, I could too. It was a positive influential moment. I needed it.

My prayer of thanksgiving was because I was always living for others and not for myself. I was approaching fifty and I had no wife or children. It was simply because I was always taking care of others. I was happy Phayla was finally ready for me to be in her life. I was happy I would have a child. I knew I deserved it. Even though I deserved to be happy, I owed God an apology. I was almost the cause of a marriage ending. I allowed the devil to show me false things. My heart was heavy. I allowed him to come into my life and cause me to give up hope. I prayed for a hopeful heart and spirit for the future. I prayed for strength. I knew I would need it to be there for my family.

Asia

It's not easy being the friend that everyone reaches out to when they are going through. I not only struggled with being there for them, but I also forgot about my husband and family because I was so consumed with their problems. Being consumed with their problems made me believe I had the solution for everything. I was wrong. I did not have the solutions. Instead of me encouraging Brooke to confront Carson, I should have been praying with her. Instead of pressuring Phayla to be with James, I should have been encouraging her to seek God for guidance. I asked God to forgive me for placing my family second. I asked God to lead me while I learned how to be a wife and mother first before I was a friend.

Katherine

As a mother, you want the best for your children. You don't want to see them hurt. You want to solve all their problems. You want to fix everything for them. I was so used to fixing things for Matt when he was blind that I told myself I would pull back when he regained his sight and became married. I pulled back the wrong way. I could have still been there for him. Just in a different way. He and Brooke struggled with communicating with each other and telling each other the truth. I should have led him to God. I should have led her to God. I didn't. I blamed myself for that. I prayed that God would take that burden from my heart. I claimed that I would pray for them and with them.

Matt

My mother was the last to pray. She ended her prayer and we opened our eyes. Tears were flowing and hugs were given. We were refreshed. We needed that cleansing.

James then said, "Hey everybody."

We all turned to see what he had to say. He turned to Phayla. He took a deep breath.

"It's time to do this the right way. Matt, can I have your blessing to marry your little sister?"

"You sure can," I smiled.

James reached into his pants pocket. In his hand was a black box. Phayla covered her face and turned away. She turned back around as he kneeled.

"I didn't think you would ask me again," she said beginning to cry.

"I love you. I've always loved you. I've always wanted you," said James.

"You better say yes this time!" said Asia.

We all turned and looked at her.

"What did you just pray for?" asked Brooke.

Asia rolled her eyes. "I just prayed! Give me a break! God is still working on me!"

"Asia!" snapped Brooke.

"Alright," laughed Asia. "Calm down! Phayla, I know you want to say yes, just keep God first and let him direct you."

Brooke smiled at Asia. Asia eyed Brooke. We all shared a laugh. Our attention was back on Phayla and James.

"Will you marry me?" he asked her.

"Yes!" smiled Phayla.

James placed the ring on her finger. The two hugged and shared a kiss. I was happy for them. I had to hug my wife and kiss her on her cheek.

We heard feet running down the stairs. We knew it was the children. Cassidee was the ringleader.

"Daddy! Mama!" she yelled for us.

We immediately turned around to see what was wrong.

"Madeline!" she yelled.

My wife and I ran to go up the stairs.

"She can see!"

We stopped at the bottom of the stairs. Madeline came walking from down the hallway. She stopped at the top of the staircase.

"She can see! She can see!" screamed Cassidee in excitement.

"Hey Madi," I said.

"Hey Daddy!" she said beginning to walk down the steps to us.

"My God!" said Katherine joining us at the bottom of the staircase.

Chapter 11

Brooke

My husband and I sat in the doctor's office with Madeline. We scheduled for her to have an eye appointment. After testing her eyesight, we were told to remain in a patient room until the doctor could review the results. For the first time in my life, I was not nervous about the results. I remember being nervous when Matt was in the hospital. It was time for me to be strong for my daughter. I could not continue to handle the situation as I did before.

The doctor knocked before entering the room. He leaned against the counter and started to flip papers in a file. He shrugged his shoulders.

"She will need glasses. Her sight is back!"

Matt and I embraced one another! We held each other so tight! We thanked God and loved on our little blessing. Matt picked her up and kissed her on her cheek.

"Let's go pick out some pretty glasses for a pretty girl."

Madeline smiled and laid her head on his chest.

Madeline sat in the back seat of the car in her car seat with a pair of pink glasses on her face. The little purple strap around her ears made them extra cute! She was just turning her head in the back seat. I smiled at her getting adjusted to her glasses.

We drove into the driveway of our home. Matt and I got out of the car. Our home front door opened. Cassidee, Braylon, and Asia were the first to run out of the door. Matt opened the back door and helped Madeline out of the car. He placed her down. Cassidee and Braylon stop running. They stopped and looked at her halfway down the drive.

Madeline smiled. "Sissy! Bubba!"

They ran to each other. Cassidee kneeled and hugged her. Braylon joined them.

"Your glasses are pretty," smiled Cassidee.

"I like them too," said Braylon.

My husband knew I was crying. My children were so loving and supportive of their little sister. He took me into his arms and wiped my tears.

"You did a good job, Mama."

"You did as well, Daddy," I said.

Matt

Not only was Madeline ally and emotionally blinded. Phayla was mentally tarnished by the actions of her parents. Her mental state controlled her emotions. She was an emotional wreck. She was unwilling to love. James too was blinded by his emotions. He wanted to love someone so bad that he could not control his emotions. He was willing to risk it all for love. Asia felt she could solve all problems. The reality was, she could not. She too needed help with her problems. My mother's excuse for not helping us was that she did not want to get involved. She was blinded by the truth. She never knew how to guide us. She thought she knew. I was blinded by my attitude toward Carson and the anger I had toward my father. Brooke was blinded by her past. She felt because Carson was a cheater and manipulator, I was too. She was afraid to return to our old lifestyle. With our love for one another, we were able to help each other seek guidance from God to see again.

The End

A Word from The Author

This is the sequel to "Love Caused The Blind To See." If you have not checked it out, please do! You will better understand this book.

Married couples experience many trials and tribulations during their first year of marriage. It will be difficult and there will be moments of blindness and darkness. It is very important to keep God first to see the light again to have a successful marriage.

You can follow me on social media!

Facebook: Author LaToya Geter-Shockley
Instagram: @authorlgs
Twitter: @auhtorlgs

Made in the USA
Columbia, SC
08 February 2023

11376792R00067